Crossing My Rubicon

Zofia Bernatowicz

Illustrated by Gayle Hesketh
and Bill McDonald

VANTAGE PRESS
New York

FIRST EDITION

Published by Vantage Press, Inc.
516 West 34th Street, New York, New York 10001

Manufactured in the United States of America
ISBN: 0-533-11650-3

Library of Congress Catalog Card No.: 95-90596

0 9 8 7 6 5 4 3 2 1

To the memory of my dearly beloved husband, Jan, who was always so very proud of my achievements and never failed to help me attain them. And to my dearest grandchildren, Sara, Clare, and Geoffrey, may this story be an example of how to pursue one's lifelong dream and face obstacles with hope, courage, and fortitude to make that dream come true.

Contents

Foreword

Crossing My Rubicon in manuscript form landed in my hands one winter day in 1994. Like many items that find their way to a busy priest's desk, it was relegated to a file tray bursting at the seams. But this case was a little different from the others as I would frequently meet Mrs. Zofia Bernatowicz and the inevitable question would be asked, "Father, have you read my manuscript?" Much like the story of the widow before the unjust judge in the Gospel of Luke, I bowed to her virtue of perseverance. To my great delight, once I started reading I couldn't put it down until I had read it through to the end.

Crossing My Rubicon is the true story of a Polish Canadian woman who grew up in war ravaged Poland and found herself swept up in the great human tragedy of that time. Living through the years of deportation and exile she found her family and familiar surroundings torn apart. During the war, Zofia became a drifting refugee, eventually landing in East Africa where she found a period of peace after the times of trouble and wandering. Growing into womanhood, her time of drifting then turned to a search for meaning in her life, eventually emigrating to Britain for career, marriage and family. Zofia shares with us the deeply human struggles of the decision to marry, the raising of children in their new adopted country of Canada and the trauma of widowhood.

When Julius Caesar crossed the Rubicon it was an irreversible step for himself and for Rome. Zofia's Rubicon was coming to terms with herself as a woman loved by God in spite of the human drama of loss of family, tragedy, personal hardship and uncertain future. A drama, however, that was filled with many blessings as she would come to see more clearly during her senior years in her adopted country. This is an exciting story of real human history surrounded by some of the great events of this century, a story of faith and hope. I regard it as a privilege to have shared in some small way in her story.

—*Niech Bedzie Pochwalony Jezus Chrystus!*
Fr. Richard Gagnon

Acknowledgments

But for my daughter's nimble fingers and her sharp eye for spotting and correcting my spelling mistakes, this story wouldn't even be written, no less have reached the press. My heartfelt thank you to her for spending many arduous hours bent over a computer keyboard, typing the manuscript. For the many hours that she allowed to be snatched away from her busy family life, I salute her generous heart.

My sincere gratitude goes to Fr. Alan Boisclair, who ordered me to write the chapter entitled "Where Is God?" which gave me a lucid revelation into my own, at times greatly confused, spiritual life. Last, but not least, thank you from the bottom of my heart to Fr. Richard Gagnon, who courageously agreed to read my story and offer invaluable suggestions. His highly praiseworthy remarks gave me hope and the courage to approach publishers.

CHAPTER ONE
Golden Days Lost

Golden Days of Summer

My earliest recollections of the events that made a significant impression on my life were around the age of seven—school-beginning time in Poland before World War II, and a very important time in every child's life. It marks the end of infancy, the early stage of childhood, and the beginning of a new and exciting era: a time

Off to School

of exploration of the unknown in preparation for the challenges of adolescence and adulthood.

I have some vague memories of my early life before that time, but those memories didn't conform to any particular or definite pattern. They rather presented themselves as a kaleidoscope of fragmented events without much magnitude, but as I look back on them now, they are very clear and meaningful to me. Like the time I was going to town on market day with my father, whom I loved dearly, and because I was subconsciously missing my mother, was doubly attached to him. Or, when I was fighting my archenemy, the gander, or picking mushrooms and berries in the forest, with my sisters.

I don't remember my mother; she died when I was at the tender age of sixteen months. A succession of three sisters brought me up—or tried to. On my first day of school, September 1, 1935, my sister Wala took me to school after sternly and thoroughly inspecting my humble attire and grooming. I wasn't too happy when she left after having introduced me to my teacher and classmates. The most upsetting aspect of that experience was that everything and everyone was so big and strangely unfamiliar. I felt so small, frightened, and unpopular. It seemed to me that everyone knew everyone else. Boys and girls were cheerful and witty, smiling and playful; it seemed that the teacher even smiled at them more often than she smiled at me. I didn't belong; I didn't want to. I was too shy, and by the end of that session I was so petrified that I prayed for something monumental to happen so that I didn't ever have to come back.

As time went by, however, things improved, as would be expected, and life at school became almost bearable. I wasn't an exceptional student, but I held my own in all the subjects, did my work at home and in class faithfully, which made me an eligible candidate for promotion from grade to grade. Then, at the end of grade four, the world around us exploded, and our peaceful way of life turned to a living hell. But about that later.

*　　*　　*

My father didn't have any particular profession or trade. In the late 1800s and early 1900s the rural population of Eastern Europe was not generally well educated. Only the privileged few could afford education. Toward the end of the partition of Poland by Austria, Prussia, and Russia, my father found himself and his young family in Petersburg, where he and my mother ran a dry cleaning business and variety store. All was well; they prospered and were very happy.

Their prosperity and happiness did not last very long though as the bloody Revolution of 1917 put an end to that idyllic life. Everything changed almost overnight. Their businesses were expropriated, even their private home was invaded by the revolutionaries. They were made to share their home with other families who didn't own a house of their own. My father, as a Polish citizen, was allowed to subsequently leave Russia. The family left just in the nick of time for, in early 1920, the border between Russia and Poland was established and "closed."

I don't know what banking practices were the custom in Russia at that time, but my father brought all his life savings—25,000 rubles—in Russian bank notes with him to Poland. These were immediately devalued, then rendered worthless in the newly forming Polish state, thus leaving my family penniless. Hence, the humble beginning!

As repatriated subjects, they were given shelter on the estate of one of the impoverished bourgeois, called Oszmiany, where my father was later employed as a coachman. This was only temporary, as in the following year the estate was expropriated by the Polish government and parcelled out to citizens who needed land. My father received his portion, twenty five hectares, to rent for life and make a new beginning.

"Oh, those were horrendous times," my father would say to his daughters. "Years of perpetual struggle and hardship." The land he had been given wasn't all arable or even very fertile. About one-third of it was a beautiful forest that was a joy to the children, some of it was given over to paddocks for animals, and the rest was covered with boulders and the stumps of recently cut trees. There was an old, dilapidated house on the property that with some effort was made into something that was deserving and acceptable enough to be called a roof over one's head. Later, that house was demolished and a new one built.

Houses in the countryside didn't resemble houses of today in structure, design or building materials. Architectural blueprints weren't required, so when the few willing relatives and friends gathered, all they needed was some wood to erect the walls, some straw for the thatched roof and some planks for the floors and ceilings. There was no electricity, indoor plumbing, or running water to worry about, so the process of building a home was very simple.

The interior would be just one large room where all the

family's daily activities would take place. If finances permitted, a house would have two rooms—a kitchen with partitioned sleeping quarters for the men in the family and a parlour with sleeping accommodations for the women. Children usually shared one king-size bed. We had had plenty of wood, so ours was a two-room house.

My sister and I shared the bed in the parlor while the boys slept in one bed in the anteroom and Father had a nook in the kitchen. Our biological clocks were so accurate that there was no need for an alarm clock and no one was ever late for anything. Upon rising, Father would go out to take care of the livestock and Wala would prepare breakfast, usually consisting of some cereal, eggs and bacon followed by coffee and milk. All meals were taken at the huge kitchen table without much ado or ceremony. The main meal was at noon, and a light supper was served in the evening. Snacks were far removed from the fancy junk food that kids are given today. I would be given a simple slice of rye bread and honey, or jam if I was lucky. Most of the time, I would just get a piece of bread. To make it more interesting I would run around the house holding the slice of bread between my teeth. My sister once asked me why I was doing this and I replied that it tasted better when it smelled of wind. So it came to be know as a *bread and wind* snack in my vocabulary—Great!

So my father became a farmer. He labored and toiled to make this newly acquired land fertile enough to be profitable, and to make ends meet and provide for his growing family. And his family was growing by leaps and bounds. There were four girls to begin with—Wladzia, Wercia, Wacia, and Wala, and a boy, Bolek, who were all born in Petersburg. My mother must have been enamored with the letter "W" for all the girls' names began with it, but years later, when I was born, she must have been at the end of her rope and so as not to tempt fate with another pregnancy, she chose a name for me with the last letter of the alphabet—Z. What a sense of humour—Zofia, as if to close the shop.

The oldest girl Wladzia had died in infancy in Russia, so only

"So my father became a farmer."

three daughters and one son came to Poland with my parents. Another brother Staszek was born on the Oszmiany estate in 1922; and since nobody thought about family planning in those days, there was soon another boy, Leon, born in 1925, and I was born in 1928, to close the ranks of our clan.

It was the infamous year of 1928, the threshold of the Great Depression that gripped the world in its cruel vise of famine and degradation. It couldn't have been any harder for my family, for we already were at the very bottom of things. We lived off the land as best we could and the only way for us to go was up, or so we thought.

My coming into the world wasn't easy, an occurrence full of drama and eventual tragedy. My birth nearly killed us both, but my mother was somehow stronger at that time and held her own. I was so small, weak, and sickly that the only thing that could have been done for me then was to have me baptised. The simple water baptism wasn't good enough as it was usually done in such emergencies—I was taken to the church to be properly baptised. The lady who delivered me cleaned me up and dressed me in whatever finery was available. The temperature that early March day was well below zero and there was deep snow on the ground. On the way to church, the lady slipped on the icy steps of the porch and promptly spilled me into the snow. That should have been a sufficient baptism, but eventually we made it to the church on time. One of the deacons stood as my godfather, and the midwife was my godmother. After a brief ceremony was performed by our parish priest, I was sent on the way to Christian life, good health, and a complete recovery.

At the Font

My mother wasn't as fortunate, and she never fully recovered from the ordeal of my birth. Her health went from bad to worse; and on the 22nd of July, 1929, four months after my first birthday, she peacefully passed away. Thus a new and most eventful era of my life began.

The whole family was devastated. Here was a large, young family orphaned and totally unprepared for life. The children's ages ranged from eighteen years to sixteen months, and in between they were seven, fourteen, eight, six, and three-years-old. At the head of this pathetically vulnerable group was my father, harried and desperately bereaved. There was no time to waste in self-pity or grieving though; reality was harsh. The practical side of taking care of a large family took precedence over grief. Reorganization was needed immediately, thus the oldest daughter Wercia, eighteen years, took my mother's place and the second-oldest Wacia, seventeen years, became assistant to my father. They shared his chores mostly outside the house and in the fields. The third sister Wala, fourteen years, took over the family accounts and the two little boys, Bolek, eight years, and Staszek, six years, helped where they could. In cases of emergency, they all pooled their resources to help each other where help was needed.

Mine was a somewhat unusual upbringing. Wercia cared for me and did her very best to replace Mother but, most of the time, I was sent from *pillar to post,* especially when the family was busy with their own activities. As the years went by, Wala and I became quite close, closer than either of the older two sisters, despite the fact that Wercia took over my mother's role and cared for me in my infancy. I was too young to remember that and Wala was my mainstay and beacon in my formative years. I also became her confidante and friend, to a certain degree.

As far as my brothers were concerned, Leon, the senior by three years, was my constant playmate. Bolek, the oldest, took on the role of observer, judge, referee and mediator. Staszek, closest to my age, was our leader. He ruled with an iron fist and was fearless. He would lead us through *hell fire or high water* and would never accept defeat or have mercy for weaklings. No pond was too deep or too wide for us to cross; no hedge was too dense or too high to be jumped over. Too bad if your legs were too short for the undertaking and you were in for a crash landing with your tender parts exposed to the brambles. My sisters, on the other hand, enjoyed going to parties, dances and on dates.

Parties and dances, at that time, would have been as simple as a few young girls taking a nice long walk to the crossroads to Our Lady's shrine to say the rosary in the month of May. Sometimes, they simply went for a walk or a swim in the river. A dance would be a gathering of a few neighbouring friends of both sexes in someone's house, where an older and more musically accomplished member of that family would play a musical instrument, most likely an accordion or a violin.

In those days boys met girls and fell in love just as they do today, but the code of morals concerning courtship, love, and marriage was very strict. Living together was unheard of and unthought of, unlike today. Premarital sex was strictly taboo and, God forbid, a premarital pregnancy was absolutely unacceptable and considered scandalous.

So when the girls went out my needs became of secondary importance. I was left to play with my brothers and their friends, whose method of entertaining themselves was not always suitable for a little girl. However, in self-defense, I became tough, giving as good as I was getting; consequently, I became something of a tomboy. This early toughness made me capable of defending myself and even saved my life years later.

Trousers for girls were unheard of in those days so I improvised by pinning the skirt of my dress with two safety pins between the legs—not very practical, believe me! Running, tackling, tree climbing, playing *polanta* (similar to baseball), skating, skiing, and tobogganing were all part of my sports curriculum. All our neighboring children were male as well so all the toys and games were of a masculine nature. Small wonder that I was unable to make friends with girls of my age in school. We didn't speak the same language or play the same games and even my dress code was different from theirs. My clothes were utilitarian in plain, dark colours and of a quality that was meant to last. The majority of boys and girls in my class at school came from the more established and better situated families, so the girls' clothes were pretty, pastel, frilly, and feminine creations. I wore heavy boots or *wojlaki* suitable to tread in heavy snow or mud, while they wore dainty lace-up boots. They were driven mostly to school in horse-drawn wagons while we walked the two kilometres in good weather or were taken in by sleigh when the weather was rough.

Polish education in the 1930s for the working classes was sketchy to say the least. The three "R's" served as the main criteria for standards of education and anyone who completed *grade four* was considered to have had achieved a good standard of education. Children were allowed to leave school at the age of twelve and work to help their families, or, finances permitting, they went to work as apprentices in their chosen trades. Building, carpentry, dressmaking, shoemaking and service were the common choices.

My sisters completed their education in Russia and my brothers, by the time I went to school, were already considered educated, and, as such, were old enough to be of some help on the farm. Help was needed badly! The farm wasn't sufficiently productive to provide a decent living for my family. The best crops that ever came out of that infertile soil were potatoes and some meager rye, oats and flax. Wheat would not grow at all so an adequate supply that would last us for the winter was purchased every year. Cash was in very short supply also and from time-to-time my father would sell some timber from our forest to the mill for paper or for railroad ties to the government. Then he could buy some livestock, farm implements, or even some new clothes for the family.

Despite the perpetual shortages and the usual struggle, there were many happy moments in our life. Celebrating special occasions such as Christmas, Easter and other holy days of obligation were such. My favourite was Christmas. So much excitement, mystery, and expectation during the preceding weeks. The preparation of colourful paper chains, toys and sparkling angels to trim the Christmas tree got all the children working hard. It was quite a challenge to see who would make the most and the prettiest decorations. Then during the last days before Christmas there would be the preparation of special dishes for the important feast of *Wigilia* (Christmas-Eve dinner).

Traditionally, there were supposed to be twelve meatless dishes such as fish in different forms, eggs, cheese, fruit and baked goods. The dining table would be covered with a white tablecloth spread over a layer of hay, which signified that the Infant Jesus' bedding was hay. In the center of the table a small, silver plate with Christmas wafers (similar to the Eucharist) would be placed, resting on the hay. After a short prayer, Father would hand each one of us a piece of wafer. We would then break it with one another, wishing each other a Merry Christmas. Then we would eat our meal, beginning with *barszcz i uszka* (clear beet broth with mushroom-stuffed pierogies). Liquor was not allowed at *Wigilia* so we drank tea, compote, cranberry juice, or milk for the children. After supper everyone gathered around the Christmas tree to sing carols and to receive a small, usually practical gift, such as a pair of mittens or a sweater. Later, the children would go to bed and the adults would attend midnight Mass.

Happiness for me was also when, on a market day, my father would take me to town with him. I would sit in the horse-drawn buggy beside him on his left. The right side he had to leave free so he could manage the horse. I was so proud and elated—for a time, I could look down on everything and everybody with disdain and condescension. I was Cinderella in her magic coach for sure. Once in the market square, we would park and he would leave me to mind the *coach* and horse and would go to do his trading. When he would return some time later with his supplies to take home, he would also bring something for our lunch. Usually it would be our favourite freshly-baked crusty bread and hot Polish *kielbasa,* some lemonade, and, of course, Polish *krowki* delicious caramel candies.

Another happy instance for me would come on Sunday, a day of rest for all the farmers. My father would take me for a long walk along the perimeter of our property and tell me stories reminiscent of the time when he was young and frivolous, living with his family on the remote farm not so very far from us. When I was too tired to walk, he would put me on his shoulders and carry me, singing beautiful, mostly religious songs. I loved that very much. He was a pretty good singer, my father.

"When I was too tired my father would . . . carry me."

Sometimes we would take a detour into the forest to pick mushrooms or berries, of which there was an abundance. *Boletus,* the king of mushrooms, was the choicest prize and most sought after. There were a number of other edible fungi, such as *chanterelles, leccinum, lactarius, rusula* and *slippery george* that were excellent for the table or to be dried and sold on market days. Wild strawberries and blueberries were used for baking, jams, or juicing. To replenish her *cookie jar* with some money, my sister Wala would take her own wares to the market—eggs, butter, homemade cheese, dried mushrooms and geese.

Oh the geese! How could I ever forget the geese, or, strictly speaking, the gander, my archenemy? There was a real hate-hate relationship between the two of us. Fierce hate on his part and sheer terror/hate on my part. No matter which way I would come out of the house—through the front door or on occasion through the window on the far side of the house—he would be there waiting. I swear that bird could smell my presence and he would attack me. The moment I heard his battle cry of *hisssssssss, hissssssss,* his long, white neck stretched to the limit, close to the ground, beak up and wide open, his beady blue eyes blazing, and waddling at what seemed like 100 mph, I would take off like an Olympic sprinter but to no avail. He would fly if necessary and always catch up with me in the end. He would pinch my flesh with his serrated teeth and beat me with his wings. Speak of an abused and battered child! My buttocks and thighs would be covered with black and blue bruises, sometimes bleeding. Desperate times demanded desperate measures so, I would refine my battle tactics and come out armed with a big stick. I wouldn't run anymore and if the stick wasn't sufficient to put him off, I would fight him with my bare hands. I would grab him by the neck with both hands and squeeze as hard as I could, watching his eyes begin to bulge, feeling his body near collapse. Then, and only then, I would release him, kick him in the rear and send him on his waddling, swaying way. After a few of these bouts, he began to respect me and wouldn't attack me outright. But I never trusted that bird and never went near the geese without a big stick.

To the geese's, and to my own delight there were many ponds and marshes on our property. I would make sure that I would skinny-dip in all of them, often all on the same day. There was one in particular that was my favourite because the colour of the water was like chocolate milk due to the deposits of fine clay on its bottom which also could be found all over our property. Once I would dry off after the swim, I looked like a negative of my photograph. My

"I would fight him with my bare hands . . . "

sister would be so startled when she saw me coming into the kitchen for the first time, that she dropped the potato masher on her foot. It was a heavy masher, by the way, in fact it was a rolling pin with one smooth end without a handle.

There are no boundaries to limit a child's imagination (especially a lonely child) and her ability to invent games or pretend situations. For me, climbing trees was an exhilirating pastime. I would scramble to the very top where I could survey the surrounding countryside and observe the activity on the neighbouring farms. Such a feeling of freedom and detachment from the ordinary gave me so much pleasure; however, such adventures did not always have a happy ending. Once, while trying to get down from my perch in a hurry because someone was calling me, I miscalculated the distance between the branches and missed my footing. Unable to defy gravity, I tumbled down. Lucky for me, my new dress got tangled on some lower branches and held me hanging there, up-side-down, screaming for help. The downside of that situation was that I was unable to escape capture and a spanking for ruining my dress, which was left in shreds.

Playing house was another favourite of mine. There were many *houses* in our backyard. Some were tall stacks of timber arranged in triangles that were left to dry so as to be ready for sale when the opportunity and need arose. I could climb up to the top without the ladder and get inside the triangle house in the same fashion as climbing up using stacked planks as steps. Once inside, the possibilities were endless. I had my toys, books, odd equipment, some food and water for a snack, even paper for drawing and writing, and, last but not least, wads of Russian devalued banknotes. I was very rich then. Sometimes I would simply sit there and pretend to be a general on the parade ground, surveying my marching legions. Or, once in a while, I woud curl up and have a snooze and nobody would ever find me there.

Quite often I was assigned to go to the pastures and mind the cows. It was a pretty boring occupation, so I would sing all day long at the top of my voice. My sister told me years later that I was well-known in the neighbourhood for my singing. Strange, because I can't sing well now.

My father had a brainstorm one day. He had decided to turn the misfortune of poor soil to his advantage and start making bricks from the clay and sand that was so plentiful on our property. Once again we were on the brink of a new venture and likely to be the most profitable one to date, if only my father's stars had been in favourable juxtapositon to make fate smile for once on his endeavours. Everything went according to plan. The bank loan was approved, material and machinery purchased and installed. Buildings were erected including an inground kiln with a holding capacity of 2500 bricks. Production commenced as scheduled. Everyone was so eager and hopeful, my brothers and father were so proud, anxiously awaiting the results. They worked like Trojans and managed to fire up twice that summer. Bricks were in great demand and the cash flow enabled my father to pay off the bank loan and prop up our sagging budget. Then disaster struck.

After an exceptionally beautiful and dry summer, fall came as wet and blustery as never before. Torrential rains followed gale-force winds. Our kiln was flooded completely, 2500 bricks that were to be ready to be fired next spring were destroyed. We were stunned; my father kept shaking his head in disbelief. The boys who worked so hard were heartbroken and resigned to give up. Life went on however, and my father, though greatly discouraged, was not defeated. Throughout that winter he and my brothers planned, sketched, and conferred with experts in preparation of the material for the kiln that would be erected aboveground. Again, all wheels were set in motion and the first production went without a hitch. Bricks were all sold out before even they were ready. Toward the end of that summer when a second batch of bricks was near completion of firing, disaster struck again. On one beautiful, hot summer day when everyone except my youngest brother Leon and me was in town on business, a sudden ferocious thunderstorm hit the countryside. One bolt of lightning struck the roof over the kiln, setting it on fire and killing the man who was tending the ovens. My father, still in town, had noticed the smoke in the direction of his property and knew immediately what had happened. He alerted the fire brigade, which came promptly bringing my father with them. It was too late though and by that time heavy rain that followed the thunder and lightning had put out the fire and flooded the kiln, ruining the bricks. *What next?* everyone was asking. The police and the doctor came to attend to the legalities of the man's death on our property and my father wasn't charged. It was judged an accidental death by natural forces.

The freak summer storm dissipated as suddenly as it had appeared. A bright sun came out as if surprised by the devastation the storm had created. Nature was shimmering in crystal-clear droplets of the recent rain, and even the birds resumed their chorus. *What was all the fuss about?*

Not *all* was lost. A large portion of the bricks were saved by the sheer force, the laws of physics. I don't remember the dimensions of the kiln, but I know that it was huge. Twenty-five hundred bricks require a great amount of space when they are stacked neatly above four huge, wood-heated ovens. Two or three tree trunks would go into each oven to keep the fire going. The fire had to be kept up continuously for two weeks, day and night, until the heat would reach the top and the top layer of bricks resembled molten lava. What an awesome sight. When the burning roof over the kiln had collapsed, a deluge of water came down and into contact with that tremendous temperature. It boiled instantaneously and evaporated, thus preventing the water from penetrating much further down.

What was there to do but clean up the mess that this recent calamity had created? And clean up we did. The crowd that would usually gather to watch such a spectacle came one-by-one to offer my family sympathy and help. So once again the wheels were set in motion to go on and pick up the pieces of our shattered enterprise.

How could one predict what the future of our family's destiny would have been had we remained in Poland? Just then, events of a horrendous nature shook the world to its foundation. Poland was the first country to take the brunt of a blow that was delivered by Hitler. Unprecedented and unexpected, the brutal invasion of Poland by the Nazis delivered a mortal blow to our nation, changing its course forever. September 1, 1939—the Second World War had begun. My childhood, as well as the childhoods of many millions of other children had ended. My golden days of summer were lost forever—I was eleven years old.

CHAPTER TWO
The Thorny Trek

Deep winter in northeastern Poland: The countryside slept peacefully under a soft, thick, white blanket of snow in predawn supplication. Nothing moved, no sound could be heard. Complete silence reigned over the frozen, wintry landscape. The woods and orchards stood spellbound, holding their breaths, their branches weighted down to the ground with a heavy load of snow. Nature paused as if in anticipation of something sinister and threatening about to happen, and, as if to order, this peaceful tranquility was suddenly shattered by a loud banging on our door. We jumped out of our beds, rubbing sleepy eyes, resenting the intrusion. My father dressed quickly and went to answer the door, to find out what all the ruckus was about. Five armed Russian soldiers pushed their way inside the room.

"Get your family and some belongings ready. You're going to be transported" one of them shouted to my father's surprised, questioning, and frightened face.

We were arrested. Our long, thorny trek to hell and back had begun. February 10, 1940, became an infamous date in history. Millions of innocent Polish citizens were sent on the road to Siberia; their only crime being that they had dared to love their country, lived for it and served it faithfully. By the end of the two-year-long *Gehenna,* three-and-a-half million perished and only one-and-a-half million emaciated individuals were saved and delivered to freedom. I was one of them.

Freedom: what a magical, wonderful, exhilarating word. At the time of our amnesty, however, our freedom was somewhat illusive, if not a baffling and overwhelming, dream come true. We were lost in an alien country, homeless, destitute and hungry. With our few meagre possessions and the clothes on our backs, we were disoriented and did not know what to do or where to go, with no one to help us, at the beginning. Our country was several thousand miles away, overrun by the Nazis who were fighting the Russians. Hitler, as Napoleon had before him, was knocking at Moscow's gates.

That was the summer of 1941, but the reality in February, 1940, was that five burly Russian soldiers stood prodding us none too gently to move quickly and get ready to go. Bewildered and very frightened, we moved in circles, accomplishing little. The news had spread quickly in the neighbourhood and my aunt and uncle who lived across from us came to enquire as to what was happening. They weren't allowed to come into the house but were able to talk to my sister from a distance. Both the women were weeping, exchanging last messages, goodbyes and requests. One of my sister's requests had been an urgent plea for some bread since Saturday was bread-making day in our household and we had none baked. My sister, Wacia, who lived in the next village, learned about our plight and came to see us, bringing some food and saying a tearful goodbye. Finally we were loaded onto two horse-drawn sleighs and were ready to go.

Irony of ironies! The *Judas kiss* delivered to us in betrayal had its immediate retribution. When the Russians had overrun our country, we had been an unknown quantity to them. Someone, usually a secret Communist Party member, would have had to come forward to denounce their own neighbours whom they considered favourites of the Polish government, thus dangerous elements to the Occupying Forces. But even enemies don't respect traitors. Those who had denounced us had been made to bring the soldiers to identify us, thus facing us themselves, and they had to provide our transport to the nearest railway station.

So there we were, a mournful cavalcade moving slowly through the countryside joined by many others who shared our fate. As we passed through the nearest town, people lined both sides of the street watching with shock and disbelief this tragic spectacle. Over the centuries, many of our people had been sent to Siberia, mainly great leaders and intellectuals, but now whole families, women and children, became prisoners transported to concentration camps.

What a shameful deed! One that should be remembered as one of the most heinous crimes of this century.

Upon reaching Konstantynow, our nearest local railway station, we were transferred to a small, local train that had been commandeered on the spot to transport us to Lyntupy, the main gathering center. The short, winter day was ending when we arrived there. In the freight section of the station, several cattle trains had been waiting, some of them already loaded with human cargo. They were sealed and a military guard had been posted on the platform outside each huge sliding door. Security was heavy as the Russians were afraid of people rioting.

Strange, unreal, bizarre—these are the words that come close to describing the scene at that station. Never before and never after would Lyntupy witness such a spectacle. Group after group of tired, bewildered people, of all sizes and ages having packed their belongings on their backs, had been rounded up and escorted by the soldiers in the dark of night, and brought into the railway yard to be packed into dark, cold interiors of cattle trains. Late into the night the loading proceeded. Traffic there resembled a busy town market day except for the mood; the generally tense and morbid atmosphere. Like a nightmare, it went on and on.

Inside the train was dark, damp, and cold. People's breath could be seen in the air. Each end of the railcar was fixed with three huge shelves that were to serve as bunkbeds. Around the walls were

"Strange, unreal, bizarre . . . "

nailed rough plank benches to sit on. Three hurricane lamps hung from the ceiling and emitted a weird, pale, and smokey light. Two giant pot-belly stoves, and beside each bucketfuls of coal completed the grotesque interior decor.

For the time being, nothing could have been done to make ourselves more comfortable but sit on our things, huddled in the middle, to prevent frostbite. The whole interior was covered with a layer of frost, even the stoves and buckets. While the men tried to solve the problem of lighting the stoves to warm us up, I had my own problems. I hadn't eaten anything that day and I was so thirsty I cried. Wala, my sister, scraped some of the ice from the bench into a cup, and melted it at what had now become a hot stove. Water had never tasted better. Then I had to have a bowel movement and wanted to go to the bathroom. Sorry, no toilets or any sanitary amenities of that kind on this train. Nature's call must be answered, however, and somebody offered us an old newspaper. The newspaper and a blanket that Wala held around me enabled me to complete the operation. This incident prompted the people around us to make some provision for such occasions. There were seventy people in that wagon and no more newspapers.

The men found an old bucket, the women provided blankets for the enclosure and we had a new bathroom, temporarily, at least. With no indoor plumbing, doors locked, barred windows too high and small, the disposal of the contents of the bucket became a *stinking* problem. However, where there is a will, there is a way. An axe was found and a hole was chopped in the floor of the railcar. This hole in the floor, within its blanket enclosure, became our bathroom.

We had even been treated to a *steam bath* that night. Within an hour of lighting the stoves, they had become red-hot, radiating an intense heat. The icy surfaces warmed up, started melting, and created clouds of steam. What a sight and what a treat! The downside of this was that everything now became damp. What was there to do but feed the stoves and try to get dry as soon as possible? I fell asleep.

It was unclear to me who was playing role of quartermaster at our end of the railcar, but by morning we were in our bunks and—oh, glory—everything had been made dry and warm. We were also moving now and on our way to the unknown. The men made bets which way we were going—north to the Arctic Circle or east to the interior of Russia. To the north were Murmansk and Archangel, where there were many concentration camps holding great numbers who were made to work in timber cutting as a slave labor force. The ones who bet we were going east were the winners, for indeed the train was heading east through Russian towns such as Witebsk and Smolensk and then north toward Moscow to join the transcontinental railway line.

At one point there was jubilation because people thought the train had changed direction and was heading west. We thought that the Russians had changed their minds and we were going back home. Some enthusiasts even started singing a hymn of thanksgiving, unfortunately in vain. It is only too easy to become disoriented being locked up, unable to see the surrounding terrain and its landmarks. We could have been circling a hill or even a town. Train stops occurred regularly but it was usually somewhere on the plains or on the outskirts of towns, to avoid offending the locals with the horrendous mess that was being left behind. Once the train was stationary and the doors had been opened, everyone who could walk jumped out into the snow under the train to go to the bathroom. Conversation between neighbours was impossible considering the circumstances. Everyone ignored the others doing their own thing and guards were very busy looking the other way.

Another reason for such stops was to replenish our water supply. Water was in great demand. Every possible container available inside the railcar would be packed solidly with fresh clean snow that would melt in the warm interior atmosphere and become an indispensible commodity for our daily use. How strong is the instinct for survival. Here a group of brutally violated people, who only a few days ago were total strangers are thrown together into subhuman conditions and adjust themselves to such a degree in such a short time that they even surprised and impressed their violators.

From day one, unwritten laws that dictated a code of behaviour for group living had been established. The people divided into two groups and bunks were assigned in each end of the railcar during the first night. Water and a wash area were in the middle by the door on one side, our new makeshift toilet was opposite, by the other door. All luggage had been placed on the floor underneath the lower bunk or under the benches. More personal belongings were kept at the far end of the bunks. Bunk shelves were about ten-feet-deep and there was enough room for the short, the tall, and the luggage. Cooking facilities were extremely limited, just the top of the pot-belly stove that was approximately twelve inches in diameter, so each family took a turn. Whoever woke up first started their breakfast, which usually consisted of some kind of gruel and tea or coffee. Our own food supplies had lasted for about a week and the Russians knew that. So during that time we received only boiling water, *kipitok,* drawn from the steam engine so that it tasted of coal, and some wood and coal for the stoves. Later a small loaf of dark, heavy rye bread was added to our rations.

Our diet was poor and grossly inadequate. We were becoming hungrier by the day as our own supplies dwindled and then ran out. We had no fruit, no vegetables, no meat or dairy products in any shape or form. The authors of Canada's *Food Guide* with its four food groups that are absolutely essential for good health would have had a fit. Bread and water for days on end. Yes, we *were* doomed to die of starvation.

Aside from being undernourished, there came a threat from vermin infestation. Unwashed, sweating bodies, most people sleeping in their clothes and deplorable sanitary conditions contributed to that disaster. Can anyone tell me where the first louse comes from? Later, they multiply like all living creatures, but the *first* one, where does it come from? Whatever its origin, they multiplied and spread like a brush fire, assaulting our poor bodies with a grim ferocity. Our clothing, hair, and bedding became so infested that lice were falling through the cracks in the bunks, literally raining onto the lower bunks and the people lying there. Nobody slept on their backs from fear that lice would fall into their open mouths.

If the lower bunks suffered from *lice rain* the upper ones offered suffocation from the heat and stench. The frozen urine around the hole in the floor of the toilet had to be deiced regularly with hot water and a scrubbing sweep. A monotonous daily routine had been established from day one without any problems or arguments. The men took it upon themselves to take care of the heavy chores like bringing in snow for water, and coal and wood for the stoves. There was always a number of volunteers to go for the bread and *kipitok* rations. While the ladies of the lower bunks were responsible for tidying our *living room* and sweeping the floor, the upper-bunk-ladies were in charge of lighting the interior. The hurricane lanterns, which were the only light source besides the daylight that came through the small, barred window near the ceiling, were cleaned, wicks trimmed, kerosene supply refilled and sooty glass globes wiped daily. The lamps were lighted each evening. The cooking and washing area was cleaned on the spot by the people who had been using the facilities at the time. There was even some degree of competition and showing off amongst the population. Cleanliness *is* next to godliness, after all.

We needed all the help we could get. To amuse ourselves, we engaged in all kinds of activities. Most ladies were busy with mending, knitting, crocheting, reading books or writing letters that were never mailed, or simply talking. Men played cards and checkers. There are many varieties of interesting card games that can occupy a person. One such game involved telling fortunes and predicting our fate from the cards. Dream interpretation was a popular pastime as well. Prayers and conversations abounded. Left and right people discussed their feelings, and cheered themselves and each other in any way possible. My sister Wala's plea to take her portable sewing machine was categorically denied, but one of the men in our railcar was lucky enough to have been able to take his accordion. He must have had a soldier who appreciated music come to arrest him, one sentimental enough to allow that man to take his instrument along. Whatever the reason, it gave us a great deal of pleasure to have a sing-along with accordion accompaniment. On some occasions, our guard would come inside to sing with us. He even taught us a Russian song, *Katuisha*. He usually didn't stay long, though, as the heat and stench inside must have been too much for him.

Once we were deep into Russian territory, our doors weren't locked anymore. Who, in their right mind, would have wanted to escape the security of a group, warm shelter and a meal ticket (however measly) to trudge into the depths of the Russian winter?

Once, in the third week of our journey, we were treated to a thorough wash in the public bath-house. We had been told to get dressed warmly, and walk a short distance to a huge, strange-looking building. Once inside, we were ordered to undress and to leave our clothing on the shelves. As if to order, men and women separated, went to opposite walls of the room to undress, facing the wall and so respecting, as much as possible, each other's privacy. The same order applied in the shower room, men on one side and women on the other. Before entering the shower room, our hair was doused with kerosene to destroy the population of lice—it works, you know. The harsh, carbolic soap that we were given to wash ourselves played its role as well to clean and disinfect hair and skin.

Our clothing, left in the anteroom, received delousing treatment by being subjected to very high temperatures in order to scorch the unwelcome inhabitants. To make this whole exercise effective and lasting, the interior of our railcars, bedding, and luggage were sprayed heavily with a strong disinfectant. We had to change our water supply quickly though, because everything was permeated with the strong carbolic smell.

We were so relieved, clean, happy and so grateful for that treatment. The women attendants at the wash-house had been mainly indifferent toward us but they hadn't been altogether unsympathetic, either. There is some good in all of us, even the enemy.

Now that we were clean, the scratching stopped and our morale improved greatly. Prayers and hopes for our safe return home were sent to heaven with renewed intensity and fervour. Although our train was thundering across the snowswept Russian plains, pushing east relentlessly, people still hoped and prayed for a miracle to happen. Those hopes were dashed mercilessly when we crossed the Ural Mountains, reaching the gateway to Siberia. The large, sprawling city of Sverdlovsk was like a gate in a maximum-security prison closing us in. We had reached the point of no return. I don't remember how much longer our journey lasted, I only remember the names of the large cities we travelled through. From Sverdlovsk the train turned south to Chelyabinsk, then east again to Petropavlovsk, Omsk, and finally Novosibirsk and Semipalatinsk—our point of destination.

On a cold frosty night, about the middle of March, in a town called Barnaul, we finally said goodbye to our train—our humble, bizarre and uncomfortable lock-up for so many days. We were loaded onto a sleigh that was pulled by a camel. What a surprise! I had never seen a camel in my life before. Dejected, tired, and very weak from hunger we arrived in Rudnik Baladgal, a gold-mining settlement that was partially populated by incarcerated individuals. Even the commandant of that area had been sent there for some *misdeeds* of his own. He still wore his army uniform in the rank of colonel with a full insignia of stars, hammer and sickle. A burly middle-aged man who left his wife and young children somewhere in the Ukraine, the colonel was sympathetic to our plight. He promised to help us in any way possible that was within his power.

Everything except freedom and the safe return home. He was a prisoner himself after all.

We were assigned to our new living quarters. They were a pitiful excuse for a house and an insult to boot. These were primitive constructions made of mud and straw with flat roofs, a low door for an entrance, with one or sometimes two small windows on each side of the door.

The settlement itself appeared strange to the European eye. It is rather difficult to describe it. It had been a primitive mining community that had grown with the availability of gold ore in the mine that had been discovered at the turn of the century. The population of several thousand inhabitants consisted mainly of *Kazakhs,* some Russians, Ukrainians and now, Poles. Houses in the large, sprawling settlement were spread across the hilly terrain, built to withstand subzero temperatures and howling gale-force winds during the long harsh Siberian winters. Most dwellings appeared as if they had grown out of the slope of the hill, or had been built back-to-back to conserve heat and to ensure stability. One winding rough road and many narrow paths went between the dwellings in all directions. There had been no plan for building houses here, no rhyme or reason for the direction they faced. All official personnel lived separately at the foot of the mountain in two long wooden structures that resembled today's townhouses.

Our *kibitka* (as houses were called) was too small to house our whole family. My father, Wala, and I took possession of that dwelling while my three brothers were housed somewhere else. The rest of our group was scattered all over the settlement. It was a temporary arrangement only, we were told by the commandant, until something more suitable could be found. Later, much later, we were given a house that had been vacated by some official who had been drafted into the army and his family moved in with his wife's parents. In the meantime, we slept in one room and cooked in the provisional lean-to. The roof above the *kitchen* was made of straw mats, where colonies of cockroaches nested, congregating for warmth right above the stove. During the cooking operation, we could never uncover the pot for fear that some of those roaches would get dislodged by the steam from their perches and fall inside the pot. Meat was in short supply, indeed, but roaches as a substitute even to us hungry folks was unacceptable.

The days, weeks, and months that followed were an unusual mixture of failure, despair, struggle, and, in the end, a triumph—but at what cost. With God's merciful help, we deportees found enough inner strength and endurance to conquer adversity and to survive. At the back of peoples' minds there was always a glimmer of hope that would never die. A firm belief that there is another path to tomorrow, another way out of this hell, was their constant shining beacon, preventing total resignation.

There was no active persecution or mistreatment of any kind that I know of to our people there. However, the sheer poverty, constant shortages of all commodities necessary for even the simplest existence, and the deplorable living conditions was enough to break down even the fittest individuals.

The commandment was as good as his promise. We all eventually moved into a new house that was a great improvement on the first one. The large, square room had four fair-sized windows, and whitewashed walls and ceiling. The wooden floor was painted with glossy deep-red paint. I loved that floor so much that I spent a lot of my spare time sitting on it, playing or reading. A lack of indoor plumbing and no running water compounded the problems of normal living. Water was brought from down below where the fast mountain stream found its bed. There were no outhouses anywhere, so the normal bodily functions were conducted at the retaining wall or at a hedge by the paths. *Kazakhs* had their own peculiar, but effective, way to keep reasonably clean. First, they would shave all their body hair, women's heads excluded. Ladies, on their way to the *toilet,* carried their own portable bidet in the shape of a copper kettle with warm water in it. On concluding their rituals, they washed on the spot within the shelter of their long kaftan that spread on the ground around them as they crouched. Men didn't even bother with the shelter. They did everything in the open including shaving their private parts.

On one of his inspection visits the commandant had tears in his eyes when he looked at me. He said that I reminded him of one of his daughters. Through his kindness we later received a cow to keep so I could have milk. A huge, black, gentle animal that I called *Czarnula* (Blackie), I sometimes tried to milk her but failed each time. Every morning I would let her out of her pen so she could join the herd that would be taken by the shepherd to the pasture in the surrounding hills. In the evening, she would return and go to her pen at the back of our house.

All the adults were ordered to work and I was sent to school. There was a flashback from my early days, something like déjà vu. My sister Wala took me to be registered in school (Russian this time), and, lo, what a scene. They wanted to place me into grade one. In protest, I went into hysterics—wild horses couldn't drag me to learn with the babies. I had been promoted into grade four in Poland when the war broke out and grade four it had to be in the Russian school, or no school at all. The teacher relented finally. I heard her say to my sister, "Let's allow her to join grade four, she will fail anyway." I vowed there and then that come what may I would not fail and that that teacher would take her words of doom back one day. And she did by the end of the school year 1940–41—I passed with four As and six Bs and I still have my school certificate with me to keep for posterity. It is nearly in shreds with age now.

Russians use the Cyrillic alphabet which has thirty three letters that are different from the alphabet in our schools. Some are the same, but they signify different meanings i.e., *p* is *r*, *m* is *t*, *y* is *u* and *n* is *p*. Before we went home that day, the teacher had assigned the first eleven letters of the alphabet for me to learn. To spite her and to show off, I learned all thirty three of them. Next morning, she called me to the blackboard to write my homework and so as not to make me feel nervous, she busied herself with the other students for a while. Later, when she turned around and saw the whole alphabet on the board, she couldn't believe her eyes. She must have thought that I copied the letters from somewhere so, to test me, she asked me to recite the alphabet. The teacher was very impressed and pleased with my work so, from then on, she treated me like all her other students.

The spoken language and grammar was an entirely different matter. Grammar nearly proved to be my undoing. For weeks on end, I would fail every piece of written work but I didn't give in. I worked diligently, and with my teacher's unfailing help, special instructions, and a lot of supplementary reading material, I finally got the hang of it. My reading material consisted mostly of simple classical stories like famous Russian fables for children and nursery rhymes. The hard work paid off in the end and I received an A in spoken language (oral compositions) and a B in written work. Other subjects such as mathematics, history, geography and biology didn't present any problems. Pride and keen application combined with hard work achieved the inevitable.

Just as my teacher was good to me, my classmates weren't. They simply shunned me, especially the girls. A foreign-looking, sounding, poorly-dressed, skinny and not-too-clean child doesn't have a chance with other children. By that time I was used to the loneliness and alienation, so their attitude toward me didn't bother me much. The teacher assigned me to sit with one beautiful little boy, the teacher's favourite and an A-student, called *Yura* (George). She told him that I came from a far, far away country, needed help and would he kindly look after me for her? He did, not by pestering me like the others, helping me with my verbal assignments when I got stuck, but mostly he just left me alone and for that I was grateful.

Besides my schoolwork, I had other important chores to attend to. All my family worked all day. Wala, always a keen seamstress, was employed as such in the sewing warehouse. Leon, who had apprenticed as a shoemaker in Poland, worked in the shoe-repair shop. Bolek and Staszek dug for gold in the goldmine. Bolek, who developed heart trouble later, was transferred to the brick-making works in the neighbouring settlement. Father, who was seventy-years-old at the time, also worked—in the stables taking care of the horses that were the main means of transport in the community.

My duties after school were those of the regular housekeeper. I had to keep our room clean, make some preparation for the evening meal, and bring our rations of food supplies from the store. There was one small store, *lavochka*, in Russian, that dealt in regular currency. The other, *zolotoskupka*, dealt in gold tokens and coupons for those people who worked in the mine. That store always had better and more expensive items such as meat and fish, mostly smoked, and some cheese and potatoes. The *lavochka* dispensed bread rations, some legumes and flour. Too much time was spent in lining up to get those supplies. Sometimes I was out in the queues all afternoon and not always with favourable results.

Years later Wala told me that one day an old Kazakh brought me home piggy-back, semiconscious from one such expedition. He had found me in a ditch near the store nearby, buried in the snow. My collar and the buttons of my coat had been almost all torn off. Some scratches and bruises on my face were further proof that I had fought and lost a battle in that line-up. What is strange, but at the same time wonderful thing is that the safety valve of self-preservation in my brain must have wiped out the memory of that

My Snowy Grave

32

scene completely. I never remembered anything from that encounter.

At the beginning of the summer of 1941 my father received a new posting as a member of the maintenance crew in the vegetable gardens that were cultivated by the brigade from the settlement. He was in charge of the potato fields and I spent all that summer with him. For months we were eating like kings, vegetarian kings that is. Bannocks and tea for breakfast and mashed potatoes for lunch and supper. Bolek lived not far away from us where he worked in the brick production industry. On his occasional visits he brought some staples for us, such as salt, sugar, or margarine, and sometimes even some home-made cheese. These were meagre supplies but nevertheless essential and a welcome sustenance. For that he took potatoes—a fair exchange.

That was one hot glorious summer. We lived in a shack made from tree branches, cooked our meals out in the open, and washed and fished in the nearby river. We built up our health, strength, and bodies during that summer. A brief reprieve that was needed so badly for what was still yet to come.

If anyone of us prisoners thought that we had been through the worst, then they were sadly mistaken. The worst was still awaiting us in the steppes of faraway Uzbekistan, at the foot of the Pamir in the Himalayan mountain range where our people would be reduced to living skeletons by starvation and disease.

When we returned back to the settlement at the end of that summer of 1941, earth-shattering news awaited us all. All Polish prisoners had been granted amnesty—we would be free at last! What appeared to be a generous gesture on Stalin's part, to release the Polish people, was in fact an act of blatant self-interest. But who cared about the reason, we would be free at last and that was all that mattered.

On June 22, 1941, Germany attacked the Soviet Union, automatically making the Soviets a part of the Allied forces fighting the Germans. The Soviets expected help from the West because the mighty Third Reich was certainly a force to be contended with. The exiled Polish government in London that had been there from the early days of September 1939, exploited that situation. The Polish Premier General Sikorski, with understanding and encouragement from Churchill, had initiated negotiations with Stalin for the release of all Polish people on Russian territory. Stalin, not having many other options, agreed. Further, he promised the following:

1 To allow Sikorski to organize an independent Polish Army on Russian territory: 100,000 men strong.
2 To supply the army with uniforms, weapons, ammunition and total upkeep.
3 To evacuate the army and civilians to Iran.

That had been a very bitter pill for Stalin to swallow, but he had had to because Hitler, with his powerful army, was now on Moscow's doorstep.

On August 14, 1941, the treaty between the Soviet Union and the exiled Polish government was signed in London by Sikorski and Majewski, the Soviet ambassador to England. The old tyrant, Stalin, had been bent a little but was not broken for he hadn't kept all his promises (uniforms, weapons, arms and ammunition came from Britain) and the promises that he did keep were delivered grudgingly and with a threatening reluctance. What's more, his scruples hadn't prevented him from helping himself to what had been meant for the Polish army. All transports of arms and ammunition coming from Britain were diverted to the Red Army arms depot. The Polish army received their full military equipment later when they arrived in Iraq. Speed and precision had become the operative words for the Polish cause, in case Stalin changed his mind.

Events of monumental proportions followed: communication was poor or nonexistent, yet somehow the news would filter through to almost all of those God-forsaken places where the Polish people were living. The password was *Polish Army—near—the Caspian Sea.* Like metal particles that are drawn to a gigantic magnet, every living Polish soul who could move gravitated towards that *promised land.* Transport after transport, with grotesque-looking individuals packed in railroad cattle trucks again were made to move south. Wrapped in rags and in tattered clothing and clutching their meagre possessions, people moved on relentlessly. Many ravaged by disease and starvation didn't make it and fell by the road.

"Many . . . didn't make it and fell by the road."

35

CHAPTER THREE
To Freedom through Hell

My father, Staszek, Leon, and I left Baladzal at the end of November, 1941. Wala had stayed behind choosing to remain with her fiancé, whom she later married. Bolek had also stayed, calling our undertaking sheer madness, considering our conditions and lack of means to travel in such circumstances. He had wanted us to wait until spring. His advice had made sense at the time, but as events later were to prove, it would have been too late then. In the spring, he and Wala's husband were conscripted. They reached the Polish army on time, but Wala and many other civilians weren't allowed to follow under threat of arrest and Wala returned to Poland in 1946.

Meanwhile in the town called Buzuluk located near the northern tip of the Caspian Sea, the wheels of Poland's war machine had been set into motion. General Anders, who had been serving his sentence as a prisoner of war in Lubianka, in Moscow, and then released by amnesty, had been appointed by the exiled Polish government to organize the army. Anders, a man of great ability, experience, and vision who didn't trust Stalin, threw himself into this formidable task with vigor, military expertise, and an intensity possessed by only the great leaders. Against horrendous odds the Polish army was organized and the strength of eight divisions was stationed temporarily in nearby towns and neighbouring locations. Reaching a warmer climate and the urgency to rendezvous with those civilians who were heading in that direction, being at the end of their endurance, was the army's main objective, so they began their move south.

To reach out and help the starving Polish population, outposts and soup kitchens were organized. Soviet authorities knew this and strongly opposed the idea of feeding civilians. They threatened to curtail the army's supplies. Who would listen to that threat?

Soldiers, who were still hungry themselves, willingly shared their food rations with the civilians. Food aid and clothing began to arrive via the Red Cross from other parts of the world i.e., United States, Great Britain, Australia and New Zealand. But the distribution of this aid created another problem.

"Soldiers . . . shared their food rations . . . "

In the confusion created by such large proportions, most of the aid cargo had fallen into the wrong hands and appeared on the black market. Those fortunate civilians, the early arrivals, took advantage of sharing from the army kitchens and medical care that was so crucial to their failing health. Bad luck and poor organization prevented us from connecting with the army units at that time. We arrived from Baladzal through Zangistobe, Semipalatinsk and

37

Alma-Ata to Tashkent at the beginning of December 1941, and the army arrived in that area on January 15, 1942. In Tashkent, the order had come for us to leave this main route and take a local train that would leave for a town called Karshi. From there, we would be dispersed to different *kolhozes*, collective farms, in the area. It was Christmas, 1941 and the saddest, most pitiful holiday season we had ever spent.

About ten families, ours included, came to Kolhoz Naukat, near Karshi, in southwestern Uzbekistan. Nine people were assigned to a one-room *kibitka* approximately ten feet by ten feet: a couple with two young children, my father, Staszek, Leon, and I, and one single man. We all slept on the floor with piles of straw for mattresses. The familiar pot-belly stove stood in the middle for heating but we had no fuel. The men quickly organized a party to go out and search for some food and fuel. They were told by the *predsiedatiul*, chief in charge of the *kolhoz*, that although he was truly sympathetic to our plight, he would be unable to help much. The Uzbekhs hadn't expected us, nor did they welcome additional people to share in their not-too-ample supplies for the winter. However, he allowed us to have some flour, potatoes, and wood for the stove. Christmas and the New Year came and went without any further developments.

Searching for work and foraging for food became obsessions. There would be days when all that we ate were large sweet onions heated in water on the frying pan. From time to time we were able to salvage some potato cuttings from *kolhoz's* warehouse garbage heap or steal *lepioszka,* a pancake resembling pita bread, from the market square in town. Those who were fortunate because they were strong were employed digging ditches or building *kibitkas* and were given soup twice a day and some flour, corn, or millet to take home. Those who had been unable to find jobs would walk to-and-fro with a look of sheer desperation in their sunken eyes and the pain of hunger in their stomachs. Under such conditions health that had been already undermined by a year of harrowing experiences failed, leaving room for the scourge of disease. Sick individuals with typhoid, dysentry, yellow fever, malaria, and many other ailments brought on by subhuman living conditions and lack of medical care, were dying by the hundreds daily.

By the end of January, after the arrival of the army in the Alma-Ata—Bukhara area, the situation improved considerably. Soup kitchens, established by the army in many different outposts and staffed by civilians, served soup and bread once a day, some dry goods sometimes, and occasionally basic medical supplies, and even some cash. Younger men immediately left the *kolhozs* to join the army and Staszek was one of them. Shortly after their families, one-by-one, followed them. Our own family kept shrinking: with Staszek gone there was only the three of us left.

At the beginning of spring 1942, father's strength deteriorated to the point that he wasn't able to walk anymore without help. His legs swelled badly at first, then the rest of his body; also, he started losing his teeth. We alerted the authorities about his health and they had him hospitalized in the regional hospital in Karshi, several kilometres from Naukat. I would walk to town to visit him each day and because I was not allowed inside the hospital, we would talk through the open window. With medical care and regular feeding, however meagre, his health improved daily. He used to save his bread rations for me so I could have some sustenance. (Parental love and self-denial know no limits.) One day, while I returned from my daily expedition, someone attacked me from behind. In the struggle we fell to the ground. After the initial shock, all my combat instincts that had been honed during fights with my playmates in my early days, shot into high gear. It wasn't my playmate I was fighting this time; this was a bigger, heavier man. No matter, I fought desperately and with all my might. I knew instinctively that I had to win or die. I wriggled, scratched, bit, spat, screamed, kicked, kneed and elbowed in all directions. I don't know how long I would have lasted had he not slowed down. He either took pity on the skinny, not too clean little creature, deciding that

I was not worth raping—or maybe the rattling bones underneath him killed his passion. At the time I wasn't even aware of the real intention of the attack. In my childishly innocent ignorance I thought that he just meant to kill me. Whatever the reason, as soon as I felt his hold on me had relented, I shot out from underneath him like an arrow, took to my wings and never stopped until I was inside our *kibitka*. After that episode Leon and I began visiting father together. A month later when father was discharged from the hospital, we were able to find a room in town and never returned to the *kolhoz*. Soon after that wondrous, if somewhat delayed, news reached us. Since the end of March 1942, the first transports of 60,000 army and civilians had begun crossing the Caspian Sea to Iran.

With hot summer weather our health and morale improved somewhat. The sunshine dispelled our constant worry about warm clothing, and by bathing in the river we were given the opportunity to keep our bodies cleaner and freer from vermin. The possibility for obtaining some fresh fruit and vegetables increased and by buying, earning, or stealing, people improved their diet slightly.

In cases where the situation would become a matter of life and death, a transgression, such as stealing food, became commonplace and even justifiable. Whether to steal in order to live, or to die—that became the ethical issue. Not that stealing would come easily. In situations like the one we were in, possessions of any kind, including food, were guarded with a vengeance. Everyone was hungry and anxious to obtain or hang on to some food in any possible way. And, it was very hard to break one's code of ethics and become a criminal overnight. There is a basic primitive element involved as well—the fear of being caught. Only sheer desperation could drive people to commit such a crime.

Apricots and potatoes had become my objectives. To protect them from pilferage, orchards and potato fields had been surrounded by cornfields. The object was to get into the quadrangle unobserved and help myself to whatever was attainable, then get out the same way and get home safely.

Once in the quadrangle, potatoes were an easy job. All I had to do was reach out stealthily with my hand to the first row of potatoes and insert it into the soil underneath the potato plant, *borrow* one or two potatoes without damaging the plant, then hide them inside the blouson of my dress. Carrying a bag was impossible, too obvious.

" ... borrow one or two potatoes ... "

Stealing *fruit* was much more risky. One day, I was up in the tree putting juicy apricots away, some into my mouth, some inside my dress. At one point, hearing a terrible yelling underneath me, I looked down and my heart froze in my skinny chest. Under the tree there was an extremely angry Uzbek with a dog. I was glad that I didn't understand his language, but his gestures were intimidating enough. Despite my fervent wish to be somewhere else that moment, there was nowhere left to go but down. I took my time, checking all the possibilities of escape. Instead of waiting until I had reached last branches, I decided to jump to the opposite side of the man and his dog. Upon touchdown, I dove into the cornfield and the rest was easy. The shock of hitting the ground and the weight of the fruit inside my dress broke the sash around my waist, unloading my cargo. Being lighter this way I could run like never before. The man never released his dog. Either he was happy enough that I had picked all this fruit for him or he had developed some admiration for my strategy and my maneuvers.

At the beginning of August 1942, the soup kitchen in Naukat's outpost closed and moved to Chardzhou, where one of the sixth infantry division had been stationed. Before they moved they advised us to leave Naukat as soon as possible. Another large transport to Iran was imminent and joining the army would be our only salvation. We did leave in the most unorthodox yet cheapest manner. There had not been sufficient funds for railway tickets, so Leon bribed two men who were transporting hay by old-fashioned means, namely by horse and buggy. Leon took the place of one of the men as a driver while Father and I burrowed ourselves deep into the haywagon in the warehouse of the hay company. Hidden thus we couldn't be seen while travelling through town, and once outside town we surfaced from the hay and spent several hours travelling in hay-scented comfort.

By nightfall we reached a small unknown settlement and the end of our hayride. That night we slept peacefully in the ditch by the side of the road, as the warm, short summer night was on our side. At sunrise we broke camp. We washed with dew, ate some bread and apricots then set out on foot to complete our *calvary*. By noon the sun was shining from a cloudless, blue sky and it became so hot that it became impossible to walk, especially since we were walking on railway tracks. Father, the oldest and the weakest, had begun to stagger and was near collapse.

Oh, where is God? With us, of course! There, out of the blue, thundering towards us came one of those wagons that railway maintenance crews use for on-line inspection duties. The two men who operated the wagon, having seen people on the line, stopped to see what was the matter. Leon explained that we were trying to get to Chardzhou. He asked them if they would kindly give us a lift since father was unable to walk further. "In you get," they said. It was a manually operated little wagon, a contraption like a see-saw with one man at each end pumping a handle up and down to propel the wagon.

Now that there were five of us in the wagon, the pumping became more difficult so Leon helped them. Upon nearing the town, our mecca, the blessed Chardzhou, the men asked us to leave the wagon so their boss wouldn't see the illegal cargo they had been transporting. At that moment—Oh Glory Halleluia!—coming from the other side of a cornfield we heard a Polish army unit marching and singing *"Wyganiala Kasia wolki"* (Cathy taking her oxen to pasture), a traditional Polish song. I will never forget that tune, to our ears it sounded like choirs of archangels.

We followed the soldiers to their encampment and finally reached our long sought-after haven. Leon reported our arrival in the camp office and the doctor came to see us immediately. After a cursory examination had been performed, he pronounced us safe and fit to travel. He had said that there was nothing that a good clean-up and maybe fresh clothes and a good hot meal wouldn't make perfect. Sick people were being hospitalized, to be transported at a later date, so everybody pretended to be well, whether they were or not.

There was no point in erecting tents for civilians as we were scheduled to leave within a few days. All civilians camped in the open air, in the shade of the trees. Actually, we left the next evening, in the dark as the army broke camp, we quietly left the area. Keeping a low profile was essential so as not to aggravate the Soviet authorities. Stalin had never been outmaneuvered, before or since, and he was in a mood to change his mind. He was still in the driver's seat.

We reached Ashchabad that same night: children, women, and old people by horse-driven vehicles and soldiers on foot. As the ship that was to transport us hadn't yet arrived in Krasnowodsk port, we stayed in Ashchabad for several days. Our camp was located in the open, on the banks of a man-made lake. Most of that time was spent swimming in the lake, walking around it, and in restful siestas. We recounted our experiences, and, of course, enjoyed wholesome meals that were served by the army's field kitchen.

Finally we left Ashchabad in the dark of night again, for Krasnowodsk, then spent the rest of that night on the sand of the inner harbour in Krasnowodsk. Later that next day, (it was the end of August 1942) we boarded a ship. What a sight, what a feeling! A relatively small ship of about an 800-passenger capacity was taking on human cargo three-times greater. People kept on coming and disappearing under the deck like it was a bottomless pit and the ship's authorities began to look anxious about the surplus, worried that to sail could be dangerous. But the prospect of a fat payoff does wonders! All passengers were told to give up all their cash under the threat of detention. Needless to say, not a soul disobeyed that order.

People were packed in so tightly that moving around became difficult, even the stairways were occupied. The situation under and above deck resembled that of sardines in cans and rightly so. The temperature below would rise quickly, heated by the engines so much so that the weaker and sicker people would begin to faint. Above deck the situation wasn't any better. There was plenty of fresh air but the toilets backed-up, flooding the deck and all our bedding. It became difficult to find a dry spot to sit down to rest or sleep. Doctors and nurses kept night watch, constantly circulating among the suffering and giving relief where it was needed. Finally around noon the next day, the Iranian shore had been sighted in the distance. We were approaching Pahlevi, the Iranian port on the southwestern shore of the Caspian Sea. Suddenly complete silence seized all passengers on the *freedom ship*. The overwhelming emotions of relief, joy and gratitude were too much to deal with. Tears of sheer happiness flowed freely down thin, tired, but smiling faces. Pale lips whispered a silent thanksgiving hymn. After so many months of heroic efforts, superhuman struggle, sacrifices, and suffering we were delivered to freedom!

CHAPTER FOUR
In the Land of the Peacock Throne

Our ship put its anchor down about a mile from the shore because the harbour was too shallow for a ship that size to enter. A few barges shipped all passengers to shore. Once near the shore, pandemonium broke out with people jumping into the water, laughing, screaming, and running to the beach to touch the ground to make sure that it was real and not a dream.

In Camp I long, narrow huts (just a roof supported by beams to give shade and shelter) were erected on the beach in preparation for our arrival. Soldiers, as usual, put up their tents in the military section of the camp and we shared their kitchen. Nobody could stay in one place, it was like a big party of jubilation. People were milling around talking, sharing news and reminiscing over common experiences.

I was so infested with lice that I couldn't stand it any longer. Luckily I ran into the lady that had shared our *kibitka* in Uzbekistan. Her husband was a barber of sorts and I asked her to help me get rid of the lice that were eating me alive. We waded into the water, away from shore, where she shaved my head. What a wonderful feeling of relief, I would finally be able to sleep peacefully at night. I washed myself there on the spot, feeling like a newborn baby.

Immediately after our arrival on dry land, my father sat down to rest and didn't move for a long time. He just sat there bewildered, crying softly and praying. Now that we were safe and sound, in the good hands of Authorities for Refugees, Leon was able to join the

45

army. From a family of six who had been deported on February 10, 1940, there were ony the two of us left: the oldest and the youngest members of a wrecked and exiled family. A few weeks later, our duo became separated also. I, who had appeared to be indestructable, finally succumbed to a vicious attack of malaria and was hospitalized in the sick-bay of Camp III in Teheran.

Before leaving for Teheran we went through a rigorous, army-style clean-up. On the perimeter between Camps I and II, makeshift shower sheds had been constructed. Upon entering the showers, all our clothes were stripped off and left behind to be burned, including all our meagre possessions, and all heads, young and old, received a good shave. On the other side after the showers, a complete new package of brand-new clothing was issued consisting of underwear, khaki-denim overalls and shoes. We became clean, civilized and oh, such happy inmates of Camp II, where we each received another package of blankets, sheets and a pillow. Several days later we departed in the army's open trucks to Teheran.

The young shah, Mohammed Reza Pahlavi, and his beautiful wife, Queen Soraya, opened their arms and hearts to the Polish people and their cause. Through their generosity all survivors who had come from the Soviet Union received the best of care in any way possible. The shah regularly visited all the camps to see to it personally that people didn't suffer unduly. Besides all the amenities and care that was provided by the International Refugee Organization, he sent trucks of fresh fruit, candies, and chocolates to the camps regularly. On his instructions, children convalescing in the hospital were taken to his groves and gardens surrounding the Royal Palace for picnics and special parties. He loved children and respected adults. His generosity was beyond the call of duty—a great man.

In Teheran people from Camps I and II were housed in brick barracks that had been vacated by the Persian military. Camp III was a forest of long, giant army tents. Inside each tent on both sides of the passage that runs down the middle, single mattreses had been laid side-by-side on the ground and made up our sleeping and living quarters. Men and women separated in different locations of the camp. We had new bedding, clean sheets and clothing, good food and loads of free time: sheer luxury—a Shangri-la!

In one of the sick-bay tents in Camp III one spunky kid, a veteran of a two-year battle for survival was now fighting a fierce battle with malaria. In a ten-year-old's body a fourteen-year-old girl lay underneath a pile of blankets racked by an uncontrollable shivering. A brave little trooper lay defeated at last. Red, burning cheeks, eyes, glazed by a high temperature, stared sightlessly at the roof of the tent. Through parched lips and violently chattering teeth I tried to utter some words of prayer but failed. A stubborn, relentless thought kept beating against my brain. Oh God, not now,

" . . . a brave little trooper lay defeated . . . "

not yet! You helped me to pull through so many times, please, please let me live now.

No amount of external heat applied to the body helps to alleviate the shivering. When the body temperature finally stops rising, only then does the patient stop trembling and relaxes with profuse perspiration and total exhaustion. Patients with severe cases of malaria sometimes have two to three such attacks a day, often with fatal results. Mine was neither a severe nor a mild case, it was just relentless. I received excellent medical care and first-class nutrition but nothing seemed to help. It was father's turn to come and visit with me daily. He would bring me some fruit, cookies, and chocolate: part of his daily ration. My appetite had become so poor that I couldn't even eat any of my own goodies. My resistance was low in a body so ravaged by previous deprivation that I was unable to respond to treatment. During the third week of my stay in the sick-bay, I was sent to the general hospital in town. We arrived there by bus around noon and somehow in the confusion of unloading, I got separated from the rest of the party. Feeling faint, I was unable to climb the steps to the main entrance so, dressed in my hospital gown, I sat down on the steps and cried. Nobody seemed to have missed me and when the time came for the morning shift to go off duty, one of the nurses on the way home came to me, wanting to know why I was sitting there crying. When I told her my troubles, she took me right in.

The hospital was overcrowded and there was a constant short-age of beds. Despite excellent medical care and an abundance of food, people became ill and died in great numbers. Two years of desperate hardships was finally taking its toll. I had been assigned to share a single bed with a girl who was recovering from dysentry. We slept head-to-toe to be more comfortable. One morning when I woke up my bed partner wasn't there and I had our bed all to myself. I was afraid to ask what had happened to her because I thought she might have died. I wasn't bothered with severe attacks anymore but my temperature remained elevated and kept me in bed. Sometime later I began to gain strength, and slowly but surely, started on the road to recovery from the ordeal. I recovered so well that I became a nurse's helper, distributing meals to bedridden patients, and other such little chores in our tent.

Meanwhile in Camp III, my father had no way of knowing what had happened to me. One day one of his younger friends arrived at the hospital to make enquiries and take me back to my father. At the beginning of December we left Teheran for the refugee distribution centre in Ahvaz, a town in western Iran near the Persian Gulf. From there people were sent to many different countries i.e., New Zealand, Australia, India, Lebanon, Mexico and Africa. Father and I were assigned to Tanganika, in East Africa.

CHAPTER FIVE

Camp Tengeru—Another Path to Tomorrow

U STOP GORY MERU, POLSKI OBOZ SPI
AT THE FOOT OF MT. MERU, THE POLISH CAMP SLEEPS.

"Little Poland" at the foot of Mount Meru

What an incongruity, it must have been some queer mistake! Four thousand Poles, inhabitants of a far-away northern country, side-by-side against Mt. Meru, a fourteen-thousand-foot high mountain and little sister to the majestic sentinel, Mt. Kilimanjaro, located in the center of the East-African mountain range. What unlikely neighbours. Even the sombre pale face of the moon in the dark velvety dome of heaven above, cracked into a comical grin. In the middle of the virgin African jungle a neat checkerboard pattern of conical-shaped rooftops covered circular mud huts—this is where four thousand Polish survivors found their refuge. Four thousand fortunates who, through God's merciful deliverance, escaped their death sentences in the Siberian hell.

Four thousand—just a fraction of the multitude that had been scattered all over the African continent and other countries of the world. There were twenty two Polish Refugee Camps in Africa that held around 20,000 people in total, mostly women, children, and the elderly. They were located mainly in Eastern and Central Africa, areas that were still under the British Protectorate during the war. There were camps in South Africa and Rhodesia as well. Their populations ranged from 800 to 4,500 people; Tengeru, one of the largest, had over 4,000. Living conditions maintained in the camps were as close to normal as could be expected under such circumstances.

World War II was being fought on several different fronts and the global community was in a tempest of political, economic and psychological upheaval. Massive numbers of displaced individuals were thrown unexpectedly into brand-new environments, however friendly and peaceful, but still as yet, totally untried. To provide normal, healthy living conditions in such circumstances was, indeed, a great task. The International Refugee Organization was performing miraculous deeds.

The six years that followed were beyond the realm of our imagination or normal thinking. What happened almost transcends reality, it was a miracle of modern times. In the heart of the equatorial African jungle, with the hot, humid, tropical climate, in

Camp Tengeru

the midst of primitive conditions, fully fledged autonomous Polish communities mushroomed and functioned like well-organlized holiday camps. Under the watchful, loving eye of our camp commandant, a retired Scottish colonel, the administration of Camp Tengeru was organized quickly and the running of the camp was performed with military precision.

To facilitate the supervision and distribution of provisions, the entire camp was divided into sections called "Groups," ranging from one to seven. One leader from each group was chosen and it was this person's responsibility to keep close surveillance over the group. They were expected to keep a precise record of all group members' vital statistics and their activities i.e., moving from group to group, hospitalization, death et cetera. They were to monitor all comings and goings and provide people with amenities that were

Old Habits Die Hard

available and necessary for everyday living. A full daily report was delivered each morning to the Quartermaster's (Second-in-Command) Office, where a precise list of food items was compiled and sent to the stores for issuance and delivery. Milk and bread were issued daily; meat, vegetables and fruit every second day; staples and dry goods weekly; housekeeping supplies monthly; bed linen as needed. The camp had its own bakery and all other food items were delivered by local suppliers and the home farm.

Ingenuity combined with fortitude and creativity was required of all the ladies in the community who were in charge of the setting up of and maintenance of housekeeping chores. Cooking was the trickiest and most arduous of all the chores. Storing food items, raw or cooked, wasn't easy because there were no pantries and no refrigeration.

Living quarters were cramped to say the least. A mud hut, approximately ten feet in diameter, housed four people, sometimes all from different families. There was barely enough room for four small camp-cots in the hut. Two were on the left and two were on the right side of the door and there was a small window opposite the door. There was no glass in the window—only a hole, two by one and one half feet, in the wall with a small door-shutter to close for the night. A tall, conical banana-leaf roof was above and there was no ceiling or floor, just a hard, mud surface instead. A rough wooden table stood in the centre with four folding chairs around it. Immediately below the window, boxes containing all our possessions had been stacked and covered with a sheet. This served well as a dresser or tallboy.

Father and I, assigned to Group Five, shared our hut with a boy and a girl of my age, children from the twin hut next door where their mother, aunt and grandparents lived. We cooked our meals on an open fire pit or in the nearby *kitchen*—a three-wall mud structure. The *kitchen* had a corrugated iron roof sloping away from the missing fourth wall, to carry away the deluge of water that fell during torrential rainstorms. Inside the *kitchen* was an open fire pit instead of a stove. Pipes *growing* out of the ground with a tap attached at the end were scattered here and there around the camp and served as our water supply. Cemented structures for latrines, wash-houses, and showers were located within each group. Hot water was provided by a wood-fed fire pit. Wood was plentiful as well as an enthusiasm and great sense of fun. Humour abounded at Tengeru. Camp comics each had their heyday and nobody complained as this was one huge holiday fun-camp.

Not that there weren't any frictions, downfalls or irritations. Some such were the malaria mosquitoes that however deadly, were at least visible and it was possible to take some precautions against them. Mosquito nets hung over each bed, and we used sprays and took a regular dose of quinine, one tablet daily. Worst of all was the assault of invisible fleas that had a dreadful habit of living burrowed under human toenails where they multiplied and spread like a brush fire. Damn the itch! One could scratch oneself to bleeding if afflicted. Drastic surgical removal of the infested toenail, together with the sacs full of nits was a necessary remedy. There would have been many mutilated toes in the camp population if the flea plague had continued. Luckily, however, after a year of so, the infestation died down as suddenly as it had appeared. Fleas seemed to accept us as the new natives of their continent.

All other ills and ailments were ably looked after by a fully staffed medical corps in the hospital that was located in a defunct Greek school building situated on top of the hill. It overlooked the west side of the camp and nearby Lake Duluti, in the heart of the volcanic crater. The hospital was a busy place indeed as many people in the camp were afflicted with malaria. Many succumbed to its relentless attacks and the harsh, tropical climate didn't help. Exhausted, too weak and unable to fight it, young and old alike rest in peace in the Polish cemetery, surrounded by the jungle forest. By now, it has probably disappeared from the face of the earth, replaced by jungle.

Not all was routine and daily duties. There was a lot of fun and organized fun activities as well. An open-air movie house, amateur theatre, and dances in the evenings were some of the activities we enjoyed. A huge library full of interesting books and periodicals, as well as back-dated newspapers was open all day long, Monday to Saturday. The lack of telephones, radios or daily newspapers was substituted by a jumbo loudspeaker mounted high on a platform on a man-made hill near the church, from which world-wide news was broadcast directly from London at 4:30 P.M. daily. One could almost set one's watch by the regularity of the stream of interested people that flowed toward the church hill on mid-afternoons.

Youths, who comprised the majority of our camp population, were organized into five different high schools according to their ages, academic standing, or preference. There were:

Elementary School
Academic Secondary School
Dress and Design School
Commerce School
Agriculture School
Engineering School

Religious life flourished and under the reverend leadership of several priests, a religious discipline was implemented with thorough determination and fervent devotion. Daily mass and vespers were said regularly Monday to Saturday. On Sunday, besides two earlier masses, High Mass was said at noon and benediction was said in the evening. Religious instruction and practice were a compulsory part of the curriculum in all schools.

Every young girl in the camp was a staunch, proud wearer of a white uniform under the beautiful sky-blue banner of the sodality of the Virgin Mary. Her tranquil holy image was printed on its folds and could be seen floating gently in the wind. Scouting, for both sexes, was another youth organization that nurtured virtuous service to God and to motherland. There were approximately 300 girl guides and 200 boy scouts. There were also numerous groups of fifteen ladies entwined in the living rosary.

Our school week was Monday to Saturday from 8:30 A.M. to 1:00 P.M., then we came home for lunch and a compulsory siesta that lasted until 3:00 P.M., since the hot tropical sun of early afternoon would not allow for any physical activity.

Going on a shopping expedition to the nearby town called Arusha was always exciting. We would have to obtain a pass from the commandant's office. Transportation took the form of a minibus that would take the shoppers to and from town. A mile or so into the woods, there was a variety *corner store* run by East Indians. One could walk there without a pass to buy things.

One day my friend and I, feeling restless, set out to walk to the store in the woods. After purchasing some school supplies and candy and feeling very pleased with ourselves, we started on the way home. We walked side by side on the narrow, grassy road on that quiet afternoon. Suddenly two black arms shot out from the nearby coffee bush and encircled my friend's waist pulling her back into the bush. The shock of the attack was so great that it nearly sent me into hysterics. While she was silent, too stunned to scream, I let my voice soar to the highest crescendo. I screamed at the top of my lungs, cried frantically for help while running up and down the road. People in the store responded immediately and even one of our gate guards from the camp came. After a few *long* seconds, my friend came out of the bushes, pale like a ghost and somewhat rumpled but unharmed. She was so upset, however, that she couldn't talk. The gate guard accompanied us back to the camp and we never went to that store again.

As time passed by, more huts were built to make it possible for people to have more privacy and to provide a hut for each family. In the process, father and I moved to Group Four where we lived in a hut just for the two of us. From day one I went to school in the camp and father stayed home doing the housekeeping. This situation, however, didn't please the authorities. Father was too old, I was too young and too busy to be able to take adequate care of the both of us. After a trial period of one year, we were moved again and I was placed in the orphanage and father was placed in the old-folks home that was located in the same camp as the orphanage and under the same directorship.

This move made us both very happy. Father had one room all to himself in one of the old-folks barracks and I joined twenty four other girls in the communal dormitory, three barracks away from father. This was a perfect arrangement. I was in with girls of my own age and same interests and we had lots of fun together. Besides schoolwork and homework after our 3:00 P.M. siesta and domestic duties assigned by our house mother (such as bringing food from the kitchen and serving meals to girls in our pod in the dining room and washing up after meals) we had plenty of free time for fun and games. Frequently, Mrs. Grosicka, the lady in charge of the orphanage, would organize and produce plays. Many of us took part in them, testing our theatrical talents, spending many interesting hours on rehearsal and on actual performances for the public. We performed in an open-air theater in the camp and sometimes even travelled to neighbouring towns like Nairobi or Der-Sal-Am to perform in a real theater. These were very exciting experiences.

For European settlers in the tropics it has always been advisable to take an extended leave of at least six weeks spent in a temperate-climate zone, now and then, to sustain good health since the harsh, tropical climate was considered too debilitating for us. But the circumstances in which we became the inhabitants of that continent couldn't allow us such a privilege. However, the authorities, who were responsible for the children's welfare in the orphanage, did the next best thing that was easily attainable—they moved us into the mountains. For the duration of our summer holiday we camped and frolicked on the plateau of the slope of Mount Meru, where the climate is much cooler and the air thinner and more beneficial to our health.

A potato farmer who owned and worked a farm on Mount Meru's slope was one of our own people, an earlier arrival in Tengeru. His two huge storage sheds where potatoes were kept after being harvested, stood empty during the summer holidays. We occupied those sheds during our stay, using them as our dormitories. Our dining area was in the open air where long, rough dining tables were placed in the shade of gigantic *tuya* trees next to the field kitchen. Our cooks from the camp would come with us to prepare our meals. We all truly looked forward to those holidays because even our diet greatly improved then, due to better supervision in meal preparation and extra funds for provisions. Our regular diet in Camp Tengeru wasn't really anything to brag about. Of course, anything was better after what we had in Siberia, but that was not saying much. Full blame couldn't be placed at the cook's door for they weren't trained or supervised properly, but I think that with the commodities at their disposal they could have used some imagination to produce better results. A shortage of supplies, the tropical heat, and probably the heat of the kitchen dimmed their willpower, drive and resourcefulness.

Our usual everyday breakfast back at the camp consisted of a large, aluminum mug of weak, milky coffee and bread with margarine. Since our daily portion of bread was very small—three small slices—a great deicision would have to be made at breakfast: whether to eat all three slices at breakfast or to have one slice at each meal. For lunch, we had a chunk of beef fried in deep fat in a big cauldron, served with boiled kidney beans and some weak, milky tea to follow. Our supper fare was usually a milk soup resembling very thin rice pudding. From time to time, the cooks would bake a cake or extra bread for our supper instead of the rice soup, and occasionally we also received fresh fruit.

During our summer holidays in the mountains we had meatloaf, stew, salisbury steak or even a roast, sometimes. We also would receive fresh fruit daily, milk, and even eggs for breakfast; that was quite an improvement enjoyed by us all. Those were happy days, full of fun, games, and small adventures. Exploring the countryside, hiking in the jungle, playing volleyball, and group singing and dancing were on our daily program. Reading books, writing letters, playing cards or simply gossiping were also our favourite pastimes. It was very difficult to return to our normal routine of schoolwork and other duties back at the base camp. Our thoughts about next year's holidays helped to ease a somewhat mundane existence.

Many friendships were made and broken during those long, fun-filled, idyllic years. I had a good friend in school, Marysia, and we shared a schook desk. Another friend, Lonia, was in our theater group and Hela was my partner in the dance ensemble. My best friend, and like an adopted sister, was Irka. Our beds were next to each other's in the dormitory and we spent many interesting hours sharing whispered confidences across the night stand. We still have a sisterlike affection for each other and write letters and exchange occasional visits, despite the fact that she lives in Montreal and I live in Abbotsford, British Columbia.

We had a pet monkey named *Miki* and she lived in the little house beside our dining room barrack. Her greatest joy was to wriggle out of her leash and get into our dormitory, where she would jump from one mosquito net to the next. Their frames were made from splintered bamboo sticks and her jumping on them broke every mosquito net frame over every bed. Imagine our faces when, on returning from school, we saw all the nets sagging sadly in the middle. Wrath to the monkey if anyone captured her! She also would steal little trinkets, such as rings or watches, and take them up into a tree to chew. Luckily for us, she could be easily lured from her tree with a banana. We loved her, but one day she disappeared and we never saw her again. It was very sad and we missed her very much despite her monkey ways.

Being a member of a scouting organization gave us scope and opportunity for many interesting and challenging activities. Girls had to pass exams in three stages prescribed by the scouting code. We went camping, picnicking and parading during national holidays. Such pride, fervour, and devotion we felt in wearing a uniform in service to God and our country. It was a great joy to watch the marching troops singing their patriotic scouting songs, their numerous banners floating above their heads. To watch proud young faces, full of youthful hope and exuberance and looking to a bright future was an exhilarating and gratifying sight.

One of our adventures involved boy scouts and girl guides on a camping trip to the plateau of Mount Meru. Our leaders, after receiving approval for the escapade from the commandant's office and permission from the local Catholic mission authorities to use the grounds for the camp, set out to reconnoiter the terrain. Finding the ground and its surrounding area safe, with water available and everything else to their liking, they returned to give us eager-beavers our orders to get ready for the trip.

On the day of the departure we assembled at the appointed place in full uniform and all the paraphernalia needed for the camping trip except the food supplies, which were transported with the field kitchen equipment. We marched in ordered formation for about two hours and by the time we arrived at the campground we were totally exhausted. We marched with our backpacks on, our shoulders unaware that we were slowly ascending to a different altitude, so by the time we reached our destination, we were out of breath. There was no time to waste on resting or fussing as camp had to be set up before nightfall.

There is no twilight in the tropics; as soon as the giant, orange globe disappeared beneath the horizon a pitch-black night took over—a very *cold* pitch-black night, I might add. The shelter of a tent, a warm blanket, and warm nightwear was a must. The proper tents usually used on camping trips were not available during wartime so we had to apply our scouting skills to improvise. We used our cotton blankets instead. Four girls assigned to one tent had to bring two blankets each; four were used for the tent and the other four for wrapping ourselves in, instead of a sleeping bag. Bamboo frames for our tents were constructed ahead of time by our leaders. We pinned four blankets together with safety pins and tried to drape them over the bamboo frames. After a few arduous hours, we had made something that looked like a tent. It wasn't much, but it was adequate shelter in good weather, at least.

After a wash, a quick meal of sandwiches and coffee followed, then we gathered around the bonfire for the usual evening scouting ceremonies. After the final prayer, sentry duty was assigned, taps was sounded, the flag lowered and the bonfire doused. We retired quickly to our tents to finally enjoy the fruits of our efforts. Sleep came quickly to our exhausted bodies.

Touch of Nostalgia

Sometime much later that night, we were rudely awakened by a horrendous noise made by one of those famous tropical storms. Instantly, our tent stopped being a tent and became a soggy, dripping rag. We four girls huddled together for warmth and tried frantically to cover ourselves with anything that was available. From the squeaks and giggles coming from neighbouring tents on each side of us, we knew that we were all in the same *boat*. Luckily for us, the deluge didn't last long; it died down as suddenly as it had appeared. Our kitchen had a tarpaulin roof so people were able to stay dry, preparing hot coffee and bread and butter which was quickly brought to each tent. In the morning, the heat of the rising tropical sun was never more welcomed. Immediately steam began to billow from our tents and clothing that we had spread on bushes to dry in the open. It was a happy ending—quite an adventure.

Besides our daily duties, such as exercises, drills, marching, and parading we had some time left over for fun and games, innocent pranks and mischief. One night, the boys achieved their wish by playing a dirty trick on the girls. For the night, our shoes were usually placed side-by-side just outside the flap of the tent. That made it easy for the boys to steal all our shoes in the middle of the night, mix them all up and line them up in the centre of the campground two-by-two, then sound reveille. As every scouting member knows, when reveille sounds, everyone shows up as quickly as possible in full uniform, ready for any emergency. Girls and boys arrived at the gathering on time except that the girls had bare feet. Well, we all know that this is absolutely unacceptable and what is worse, that is a punishable offence. Despite the surprised and stern-looking faces of the leaders, we weren't penalized for our misdeed. The incident was explained and treated as a big joke.

The girls planned a revenge but couldn't carry out their threat. We were supposed to steal the boys' pants and sew the pant legs together, so they would arrive at the gathering in their underwear, but the plan never came to fruition. After our fiasco the boys were on their guard and it was impossible to steal anything from them, and, of course, the trumpeter wouldn't sound reveille for *us* anyway.

On Sunday we attended a mass in the nearby little old church. Mass was said in Latin but the hymns were sung by the natives in their own dialect. It was a beautiful, haunting, melodic chanting that went straight to one's heart and soul. After a few days of those refreshing adventures, we returned to the base camp feeling proud and grateful for the exciting time we had had.

Thoughts about our homeland, however far off it lay in the distance, were never far from our minds. A plea for a free and independent Poland was always sent to the Almighty in our daily supplications. Fervent prayers were also sent to heaven for the safety and fortitude of our troops fighting on Italian soil, laying down their lives in the battle for the freedom of the world community. The German aggressor, who so brutally overran our country and half of the world, was now in desperation facing Armageddon for his shameful deeds on Monte Cassino.

*   *   *

A free and independent Poland—what a dream! Little did we know that in reality it was never to be, that it would remain just a dream, an illusion. How is it that with the stroke of a pen, with the raising of two fingers in the *V for Victory* sign, that the fate of a once-great nation, an empire that stretched from the Baltic to the Black Sea, could be wiped off the map of Europe? A nation that in the seventeenth century so staunchly and bravely defended Christianity against the onslaught of the infidel Turkish hordes—how is it possible that the hope of our troops in Italy (who had their own fantasy of a trimphant arrival in their tanks on free Polish soil) could turn to dust? How is it possible that the world's battle cry "For our and your freedom!" could lose its noble meaning? Yet it did.

In 1945, at the end of World War II, for the sake of expediency and so that the rest of the world could enjoy peace, half of Poland was signed away to the Soviet Union. The iron curtain, a new phrase, was coined for the vocabulary of history. The other half of Poland, was ruled as a Soviet satellite state, by a sham Polish government appointed and dictated to by the Soviet Union.

It was useless, however, to wallow in self-pity; we had been betrayed once more. No free Poland, no country for us—it was as simple as that. It is not very wise to return to a country where one has been violated once already and is still governed by the same ruler. The world was wide enough and we decided that we could be happy campers somewhere else. The cruel, ironic twist of history that shaped Poland's fate after the war hadn't come as a total surprise to the Polish population. Our faith that there would be a bright future ahead, that after so much suffering and sacrifice all would be well, was quickly destroyed. That bright hope had been thoughtlessly dashed and the bright future of a free Poland denied to its people.

The untimely, mysterious, and tragic death of General Sikorski, the Premier and head of the exiled Polish government, in an airplane catastrophe over Gibraltar in 1943 had already cast a premonition of doom over the Polish community scattered all over the world. A feeling of approaching disaster and the collapse of the Polish cause became almost inevitable. Two years later, harsh reality justified our premonition of gloom and doom. We lost our country for the second time in this war to become *pilgrims on an unending road.*

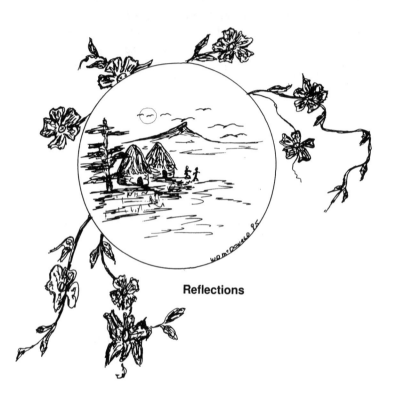

Reflections

CHAPTER SIX
Rolling Green Hills of Devon

In June 1948 we left Africa and were transported to England to be reunited with our brothers and fathers who had fought in the war. Our departure from Africa had been uneventful; we left Camp Tengeru by train in the middle of June 1948 and arrived in Mombasa port where we boarded a passenger liner named *Carnarvon Castle.* After a pleasurable two-week-long voyage through the Red Sea, the Suez Canal and the Mediterranean we arrived in Southampton port in the south of England.

My friend Janka and I enjoyed each other's company *cruising* for two weeks on that voyage. We also ran into two more friends from our orphanage, Kazia and Ludka, two sisters who later became our inmates in barrack number sixteen in Daglinworth, and inseparable companions on the train trip to Stover Park Hostel in Devon, our final destination.

The tender loving care of the International Refugee Organization had ended with our arrival in England. We were taken over by the British authorities to be eventually transferred to the normalcy of free living status of political refugees at a later date. Janka left Stover Park soon after our arrival to be reunited with her foster father. Our military had preceded us by two years. At the end of the war, after spending some time in Italy dismantling and liquidating the war machine, our troops were brought to England in 1946 where their units were demobilized. By the time we arrived from Africa in 1948, most of the men were already in civilian life, working, and eager to meet with girls of their age to date and marry.

In the meantime, we were taken from Southampton by train to the transient camp in Daglingworth near Cirencester in the county of Gloucester where we spent two weeks waiting for a final dispatch to a permanent destination. Stover Park Hostel in the beautiful, breathtaking rolling hills of South Devon was our lot—what luck! We lived near the Queen of the British Riviera (Torquay) for the next thirteen years.

They were highly challenging years and the most interesting, happy, fulfilling and productive time of my life. A whole new horizon of possibilities arose to entice, and quite often perplex, young eager fledglings of our so-ravaged generation. Meeting and dating men was an especially delicate matter to deal with. Growing up in a war-torn world, where the moral fabric was nevertheless based on a Victorian-era mentality, gave little positive rules to go by. To establish and maintain a normal boy/girl relationship accept-able to both sides required a great deal of ingenuity and diplomacy. I personally knew nothing or very little about sex and, even then, mostly just distorted tidbits. The fact, that at fourteen I was shocked almost to death at my first monthly period, illustrates my point. I was so ashamed that it had appeared that I did something dreadful, I contemplated drowning myself from shame. Halfway down to Lake Duluti I lost my nerve, got scared of dying, turned back and came to my father to tell him a lie, that I hurt myself climbing a tree and that was why I was bleeding now. He was shocked and ashamed of his neglect, more than I was at my predicament.

But that was many years in the past, now I was twenty years old and I felt like the world was my oyster. It was time to begin dating and think about marriage and family life. A new life in England was so enticingly exciting and so different from any life before that. Eventually, all the difficulties and obstacles would be overcome and misunderstandings between new friends explained.

Kazia, Ludka, and a new friend, Zenia, were my constant

companions. We went to parties, dances, and movies in town together, savouring our newly found freedom and maturity. We also all worked in the woolen mill in Buckfastleigh. Ludka and I are still on sisterly terms. She lives in Toronto with her family and we spend occasional holidays together, write letters and talk on the phone.

For the next two to three years, churches and registrars were busy indeed. Marriages were performed with speed and new family lives established with efficiency. Thus, a new post-war Polish baby-boom generation became a reality.

As for me, after two or three dates with different men in the first year, Jan and I met and fell in love. It wasn't love at first sight, but we liked each other very much at our first meeting. We corresponded during the next year since Jan lived and worked in the Midlands. Frequently he came to Stover to visit with his family, who also lived in Tengeru, Africa. His two sisters, Hania and Janka,

Jan Came Courting

attended the same school in Tengeru as I had and we also were in the same Girl Guide Troop.

In the early spring of 1950 my private world was badly shaken again when my father, after a brief illness, passed away, leaving me devastated and stunned by the loss. We had been through so much together and now he was gone. It was the passing of an era and I was desolate. Jan proposed to me that spring. I accepted the proposal eagerly and we were married on August 8, 1950. That was a turning point in my life—a straight new path lay ahead.

Ours was a beautiful wedding and will always stand out in my memory as the happiest day in my life. Five of my friends and three of Jan's sisters were my bridesmaids and their escorts were in my bridal entourage. It was a memorable day, full of truly youthful celebrations and so many good wishes for the future. For me, it was an extra-special occasion because it was such a communal effort. Hard post-war times didn't exactly abound in the luxuries and amenities that people enjoy today. Kazia, an accomplished dress-maker, made my wedding dress. Zenia was responsible for the arranging of my bridal bouquet and veil. Jan's mother and her friend made tortes, cakes, and doughnuts. I was in charge of stuffing and roasting the chickens and also of boiling a ham. Jan and his crew arranged tables and provided liquor. Ludka lent me her expertise in slicing and arranging meat platters and salads. In the morning, on the day of the wedding, all my entourage assembled in the reception hall (an empty barrack), to do all the final preparation for the food and decorations for the wedding dinner, later in the afternoon, after the wedding ceremony.

By marrying Jan, I also acquired a whole new family, four sisters: Hania, Janka, Marysia and Halina, a brother, Staszek and both parents. I was accepted with open arms and after having just lost my father, it was a welcome situation. Becoming a member of a large close-knit family was so reassuring and helped me to overcome my grieving.

For the majority of young girls of my generation, a virgin

bride, handsome husband and motherhood represented the pinnacle of life's achievement; a career was of secondary importance. Everything seemed to be coming together. Jan and I worked very hard the first year, which enabled us to equip our home and provide better conditions for the children that we were hoping to have. Our hopes were realized when, on July 12, 1952 our first born came along, a little girl we named Krystyna Maria. When Krys was about eight months old, Jan's parents agreed to look after her so I could go back to work, to supplement our income.

Life in post-war England wasn't easy. Damaged by the war, the economy was slowly gathering momentum on the way to recovery. Although jobs were plentiful the wages were low. Consumer goods were scarce and of an inferior quality. Housing presented the most grief and hardship. Ex-soldiers and their families who arrived from Africa, were housed in the camps that the American Forces occupied during the war. Stover Park, which our group took over, had served as a general hospital for wounded American soldiers. Existing facilities there were perfect for the families that had members who were old, frail, or sick. Beatuiful surroundings like the green velvet of the nearby golf course, large deep lake and typically English oak forests around the camp and a moist, mild climate, completed a perfect picture compensating for the uncomfortable and inadequate living quarters.

There were no cooking facilities for individual households. A communal kitchen provided meals for the whole camp population. Three meals a day were served in the dining room adjoining the kitchen. The sick-bay had meals-on-wheels and brown-bag lunches were provided for people going out to work. Gradually, however, encouragement for decentralization became a frequent occurrence. Younger families, as well as newlyweds, were provided with larger rooms where cooking ranges were installed. Some luckier ones received council-housing, while others left for other parts of England to be reunited with their families.

Despite the usual drawbacks and irritations of daily life,

71

happiness was unquenchable. Nothing could dim the enthusiasm and joyous exuberance. We lived in one room, 14′ by 14′, where we slept, cooked, ate, and played. We couldn't afford a new double bed so we enlarged my single bed with a plank. Underneath, the bed space was used for storage. There was no stove in the room so we used a one-burner portable gas stove for cooking our meals. A small pot-bellied stove provided a source of heat in the winter.

When our daughter was born, we moved to a larger room, 14′ by 20′, with a cooking range fueled by coal. Ours was a good marriage. Although we both weren't of the clinging, hand-holding types we were very, very close, supporting each other, and doing everything together.

Housekeeping chores like shopping, cooking, and looking after our daughter after work and on the weekends were a fifty-fifty arrangement. We did a great deal of travelling by bus, with our little one in our arms. We often even went to the movies and most of the time, Krys slept through the whole performance. Trips to the zoo, seaside towns and fun-fair in Newton Abbot or Torquay were on our permanent social programme. Life was so good!

Krys would have been considered spoiled little Miss if there is any truth in the experts' popular opinion that spoiled children grow into deliquent adolescents, and even sometimes, into criminal adults. Nothing can be further from that claim in her case, and she was spoiled endlessly from the moment we brought her home from the hospital. There were nine adults in our household who went "ga-ga" when she was born. Besides Jan and me, there were grandparents and four of Jan's sisters and a husband of one of the sisters who constantly were on hand to give their attention to the little newcomer. There was no way to escape each other's company because we lived in the same barrack. Sometimes, Krys would be so wound up by the end of the day that it was difficult to settle her down for the night.

There was no shortage of playmates, either. Young mothers, some of them my own friends, all were having babies and were only too eager to show off their cuties and to compare notes on their development. One of them was my friend Hela whose two daughters, Violetta and Renia, were the same age as Krys. They were Krys' best friends for the duration of our stay in the Hostel, and Hela and I spent many languid, sometimes anxious moments watching our brood, who played in a sandbox, frolicked in puddles, or pulled each other by the hair. All children in the camp spoke Polish, so to prepare them for their entry into English schools, a preschool was organised in the camp where the teacher spoke English with them, taught English nursery rhymes and sang English songs. As children learn quickly, by the time they entered the English school system they were proficient in that language and had no problems in communication.

Thanks to our Hostel priest, Fr. Galzewski's patronage and intervention, many of our children from the camp were enrolled in the nearby convent school at a very low tuition cost, just a token payment of nine pounds a month, and Krys was one of them. I began my course of study at the technical college that same year, so mother and daughter left the house each morning to go to school together. I would see her off on the school bus at the camp gate and catch the red Devon General bus to go to the city on the road outside the gate. After school, her grandparents would meet her and take care of her until Jan returned from work. My classes ended at 5 P.M. and I would return home around 6 P.M. By then, Jan would have begun preparations for our supper and played with Krys. Krys' cousin Basia who lived in the next door barrack was also her eager playmate. Amicably they shared their toys, interests, and adventures. Basia was a lovely, gentle little girl who had a calming effect on Krys' livelier disposition. Their natures complemented each other perfectly.

One incident from Krys' childhood that touched our hearts in a special way was the plea that she sent to God on the day of her First Holy Communion. When the priest asked her what would be her most earnest wish that she wanted God to fulfill her answer was,

"I want my Mum and Dad to become saints." That truly surprised the priest and made us very proud, humble, and grateful parents.

Little by little, the population of the Hostel began shrinking and many moved into towns, finding lodging with English families. A great many emigrated. To buy a house in town was impossible because nobody could save a sufficient amount of money. Non-citizens weren't eligible for mortgages and to acquire British citizenship was next to impossible. More room became available now: we had two rooms and a box-room for storage. Washrooms, a bathtub, and a laundry room were shared by all the families in the barrack. As things started to change around us, we became restless also. We thought about a more solid future and the betterment of our living conditions.

Prospects for a better job became of paramount importance and after numerous discussions, we decided that returning to school was a must to acquire a trade. Jan was working as a labourer on a construction site in Newton Abbot and I worked as a mender in the woolen mill in Buckfastleigh. With some soul-searching and deliberation, we decided that I, as the lower wage earner, should go to college. Teaching was my choice, but the nearby technical college didn't have a teacher training program, so my next choice was a three-year Hotel and Catering Business Administration Diploma Course.

Entrance to the college was no problem. My Polish high school certificate that I had acquired in high school in Africa, translated and transcribed, was accepted with the English General Certificate of Education "O" Levels. Financing the course and withdrawal of my wages from our household budget was a problem, however. I applied to the ministry of education for a grant. I received forty-four pounds a year from London for textbooks, free tuition for three years, a travelling pass and ten pounds per year pocket money from the local Education Authorities, in Exeter. That was more than generous.

There was a great challenge ahead of me! My proficiency in

the English language wasn't very good, but I must have impressed my interviewers at the ministry and head of the department at the college sufficiently to be accepted. I worked very hard during those three years and even harder during the summer holidays to prop up our finances. If it hadn't been for Jan's unfailing help with our household duties, parenting, and moral support, I wouldn't have been able to do it. He even helped me with my school work, sometimes rewriting my notes or doing engineering drawings for my assignments.

My studies at the college were more than a challenge; they were a formidable task to accomplish. I had to compete with other students in the course who were all recent high school graduates with fresh minds, and eager, youthful approaches to school work. They were also sons and daughters of hotel owners and were familiar with the rudiments of hotel business administration. Competition was fierce and school, at times, seemed almost an insurmountable undertaking for me. I was the only mature student and a foreigner to boot. I was something of a catalyst insofar as my presence spurred others to work harder to beat me. With the language barrier a "monkey on my back," I had to study harder. All final theory exams came from the city and guilds of London, where we were just numbers to those who examined our papers. Practical exams were also adjudicated by an examiner sent by the ministry of education, but the college exams were easier. I received a great deal of help and understanding from the instructors but, although sympathetic and extra helpful, they were in no way lenient in grading me. To overcome my language shortcomings in the first year, I learned almost all my lessons by heart and at the end, passed all my exams with flying colours. Great!

In 1957, Mary, one of Jan's sisters, emigrated to Canada to join her fiancé and to be married soon. From then on, requests for Jan and me to come to Canada began in earnest. Mary and her husband owned their own business and needed good, reliable workers. They wanted Jan to work for them as a carpenter. We were reluctant in the beginning, subconsciously still hoping that we might return to Poland. We didn't want to go so far away from the family, either. My entering college in 1958 put off thoughts about any moves or changes for the next three years.

However, after I graduated in June 1961 there were no more excuses for the delay. Just to "test the waters," so to speak, Jan left for Canada in September 1961. If he like Canada, then he was supposed to work long enough to make enough money to enable him to pay for our passages to Canada, but the wages were still so low then. Too impatient to wait for too long, he took a loan from the bank to pay for our airline tickets.

Krys and I arrived in Canada on November 11, 1961. So! There was another new life's chapter opened before us. I was so moved at the airport that I cried when the emigration officer, after greeting me warmly, handed me a family allowance cheque for Krys for eight dollars. The gesture was touching, a never to be forgotten experience.

CHAPTER SEVEN
Pilgrims on an Unending Road

Now comes the hardest part of my writing venture. To give negative accounts about the country that you hold in the highest regard is such a difficult task. It goes against the grain, and my basic principles. Canada: I believed it to be the most beautiful, colourful, plentiful, most sought after and dreamed about country in the whole world. Paradise on earth! And as it was in that other paradise in biblical times that there was a serpent in it, this Paradise had a giant deadly W.A.S.P. It stung and stung and stung. Its venom was so lethal that it nearly killed me.

One would think that having a trade and being prepared and eager to work hard in a country where at the time, jobs were plentiful, would not make it so difficult to find a job. But for me, it was next to impossible. A difficult name to pronounce, accented English, a foreign education, were all strikes against the odds of obtaining or holding a job.

To go into details about it would be too painful and in bad taste. The only thing that should be said is that it was sheer ignorance and lack of Christian charity of those individuals, who so readily perpetrated those acts of persecution and harassment in the workplace. I can find enough compassion in my heart to forgive them and hope that they can forgive themselves. I'm overwhelmed that they can live peacefully with such shameful deeds on their consciences.

Things improved as the years went by. I met and worked under many wonderful people of the same profession and rank who were a shining example of decency, hard work and professionalism. A most redeeming feeling that restored my faith in the human race.

For our first twelve months in Canada, we lived in an apartment in North Vancouver saving hard from our wages so we could buy a house. After several arduous weeks of trying to get a job, I managed to get a waitress' position in the newly-opened hotel on the North Shore. My starting wages were ninety-five cents per hour and Jan's were one dollar and fifty cents per hour. It was difficult to save quickly to buy a house although house prices were very low. We applied and got a mortgage and bought a lot for a very low, special price from Jan's brother-in-law Andy and had our house built.

My First Job in Canada

In September 1963 we moved into our own home. Our own

first house after so many years of wandering around the world. Can anyone understand the feeling of solemnity and gratitude of the vagabond who comes home at last? The survivors of a global upheaval, reaching the safety of a peaceful haven. Such moments are hard to describe as well as comprehend by individuals who have never experienced such events in their lifetimes.

Months and years rolled past. Life was good but not always easy. We juggled our daily activities so we could work and look after Krys, who was now eleven years old. I took on split shifts in the hotel dining-room so I could drive Krys to and from school, look after her in the morning, make dinner then it was back to work on the evening shift when Jan returned from work. There were times when we passed each other on the stairway, he coming home and I leaving. Sometimes, I would return around midnight and Krys and Jan would be fast asleep by then. We never complained, being grateful, and drew satisfacton from the achievements of our modest but productive life.

Not being able to afford holidays away from home, we travelled a great deal locally on day trips. We went to the zoo, parks, beaches, and to the movies in town. Our first holiday was in 1965, a week in a fishing camp in the Interior where we shared a cabin with our brother-in-law Andy and his wife Mary who had a standing booking there each summer.

Krys was an exceptionally good child. She never gave us any grief or anxiety—the usual teenage generation problems. Without working too hard on her school work, she was promoted from grade to grade with commendation. We never experienced any trouble or hardship because of her in school or at home. Her demands for clothes and entertainment were also modest—in line with the availability of funds and our income. She didn't smoke or drink and her greatest joy was to have her three school chums, Susan, Diane, and Valerie over for a sleepover in our home. They spent most of their free time together watching T.V., listening to records or playing badminton. They all graduated from high school in 1970.

As a treat she and I went on a trip to Europe that for a year we had been saving hard for with the credit union special holiday fund. I went to Poland to be reunited with my sisters who I hadn't seen for almost thirty years. Krys went to Devon, England to spend time with her grandparents, cousins, aunts and uncles while Jan, by his own choice, stayed home.

Krys' love life was on an even keel also—almost spartan in its quality. There were one or two boys next door, just friends, who walked with her to school and carried her books sometimes but nothing serious, just casual acquaintances. After graduating she attended university to study education and worked on weekends in her aunt's store. There she met a young man, the security guard in the shopping centre, with whom she fell in love.

It was love at first sight and they married at the end of that year. This left a terrible, painful void in our lives: the sadness and coldness of an empty nest. We wish our children all the best, we want them to grow up and marry, but when the time comes for them to go, we almost grieve their leaving. Perverse human nature!

Thoughts and hopes about the "pattering of little feet" alleviated the cold comfort of the empty nest. We were tried sorely on that one, though as there was no sign of pregnancy for the next seven years. Our first grandson Geoffrey, was born on November 7, 1978. It was an explosion of great joy and jubilation! I never imagined that one can love a child with so much intensity. It felt like Jan and I were in love all over again. Two more grandchildren came along, born five years apart, first Clare, then Sara. We love them all very, very much, each one in a different way.

In 1981, Jan's bosses decided to retire and they sold their business to another company. Jan and some other employees went to the new company along with the inventory. Nineteen eighty-two ushered in a crisis in the labour market and Jan, with many others, fell victim in that recession. He was recalled the next year, but the situation worsened. In 1984 his company went into receivership and then went bankrupt. Jan received automatic preretirement unemployment benefits and the following year, at sixty five years of age, he retired. I kept on working as a food manager in a long-term care facility.

Although Jan and I were both working all the time, we hadn't saved much or not as much as we should have. The children were in financial difficulties now and then and we kept helping them unfailingly. All for the best, we still had enough left for a comfortable living and some savings leftover. After three years of working in one of the long-term care facilities, I was fired. The reason for the dismissal was that I hadn't come up to their standards. A blatant injustice! In fact, it was I who was unwilling and unable to lower my standards, to act against my principles, and to disregard work ethics. During my three years in that facility and my unblemished record, I passed the scrutiny of the accreditation commission with honours for my department. My title as director of dietetics stands on the files and on the "two-year accreditation certificate" that was awarded to that facility. Now, does such a record warrant dismissal?

There was no reason for us to stay in town any longer since the country was where we always had preferred to live. So, we bought our new home in Clearbrook and moved to the Fraser Valley in 1985. Unable to find work locally, I accepted a position of food manager in a long-term care facility forty-five kilometers away. While the work was perfect, driving to and from work on dark frosty winter mornings and evenings wasn't; to beat the rush-hour traffic on a snowy, icy freeway takes a great deal of stamina and steady nerves. After four years of this gigantic effort, I couldn't face another winter of driving and resigned my position at the end of September 1990 to stay home. I hoped to find something suitable locally.

CHAPTER EIGHT
Gone Is My Camelot

My search for work locally proved fruitless, and in the meantime Jan's health began to fail. Over the years, he had been warned repeatedly by his doctors to stop smoking, to at least minimize the number of cigarettes he smoked. Their advice and my pleas fell on deaf ears. He continued to use some medication and an inhalator to ease his smoker's cough, with little result. Around Christmas that year he caught some kind of virus. Bad coughing and a slight temperature followed, but he didn't take it seriously and would not see a doctor, despite my nagging. "It's nothing that a couple of aspirins and some cough syrup won't cure," he would say, telling me I worried unnecessarily. He improved slightly over the Christmas holidays but the cough continued.

After the New Year, I had my checkup and I begged Jan to come with me to that appointment. He agreed. Once in the doctor's office I told our doctor that I was concerned about Jan's cough and asked him to check Jan out thoroughly. A chest X ray showed a spot on his left lung; results from a needle biopsy were positive: Jan had cancer in his left lung. The horrendous verdict, given by the doctor with clinical precision, had the whole family shaken to the core. First disbelief then helpless surrender followed. What could be done to prevent the spreading of this dreadful disease? Everything, to our knowledge, had been done that was possible.

Events followed one another quickly. Procedures, tests, visits to specialists were ordered and attended. A thoracotomy and lower left lobectomy were scheduled for April 1, 1991. The surgery lasted seven hours and his recovery was successful. I brought home a thinner and somewhat weaker Jan after a ten-day stay in the hospital. The doctors said the prognosis was good, the healing of external wounds was as good as could be expected, however, the pain continued inside his chest when it should have already subsided.

Obviously there was something very, very wrong. The doctors either didn't know for certain or weren't telling us the truth. At the end of June when he felt stronger, Jan underwent twenty sessions of radiation treatment. He was expected to improve, to feel better, but he didn't and the pain in his side persisted. The debilitating effects of the radiation alone took their toll.

I knew then that I was losing him. It was just a matter of time. Needless to say, we spent all that time together, the little precious time that we knew we had left. At the beginning of August, Jan developed a high temperature and hyperventilation. I took him to the emergency room where the doctor's verdict was acute pneumonitis. Antibiotics, and finally steroids were prescribed, and these definitely picked him up. His appetite improved, he suddenly felt stronger and seemed brighter, even the pain subsided. We were jubilant that the right medication had been found finally. There was a catch, however. As long as he stayed on high doses of medication, he felt fine, but he seemed to require higher doses to maintain this feeling. Prescriptions were renewed and therapy repeated three times. Finally, his doctor said, "No more steroids, we are not getting anywhere this way." Without the medication, Jan felt poorly, he was really ailing. Three days later, on December 2, 1991, he collapsed and was hospitalized. On December 19, 1991 he peacefully passed away. My private world halted and crumbled at his bedside in Room 224.

The blow was so great, the helplessness so irrevocably devastating that I thought I would never feel normal and whole again; that the hollowness in the pit of my stomach would never shrink and allow me to breathe normally again; that the deluge of tears that flowed freely when I was alone would never stop. My face and eyes had become so swollen that I couldn't recognize myself in the mirror. We quite often hear and quote cliches like "my world went to pieces, my universe collapsed, my dreams turned to ashes." There is a frightening truth in these cliches, though not in the literal sense. My physical body remained the same, the world around me hadn't undergone any changes. But my mind, my inner self, became so fragmented that I couldn't formulate a coherent thought for some time. Actually, some form of disorientation assails one's mind in grief. Instead of one whole person, there are two almost separate entities who take over. One that walks, talks, and tries to behave normally, attending to practical necessities and functioning almost automatically. The other one, overcome by tragic emotions, surrenders to grief and pain completely. Two selves, unable to fuse and function as one, create turmoil and chaos in one's mind. Pain persists and increases as the shock of the tragedy subsides and is replaced by the realization of the enormity of the loss, of the mournful prospects of a lonely and desolate life that stretches ahead.

The pain is so acute, the helplessness so complete that it almost bordered on panic as I listened to his last long, deep breaths, each one with a longer pause in between. It is impossible for me to tell which part of me died with him, but I am certain that I perceptibly changed at that moment and can never heal completely. The atmosphere around us underwent drastic changes also.

For two weeks, day and night, there was so much activity in his room: nursing staff moving around, attending to his needs. I was there talking to him and *for* him, as Jan lost his voice about two months before dying. The rest of the family and friends came visiting. The forest of IVs, at least three on each side of his bed, and the constant, enervating hiss of the oxygen that assisted his breathing. Suddenly everything stopped and the silence was deafening. I was reluctant to leave him; it is frightening to make that break, to take the first step into completely new territory—like being in a twilight zone. A new life of diminished capacity, lowered status, a widowhood that is a bitter, burdensome title that the bereaved spouse acquires. Jan died at four o'clock in the afternoon and at 7 P.M. I still lingered by his side. Mary, his sister, stayed with me as Krys had to return sooner to the children, whom she had left at a friend's house.

When a nurse, looking in for the third time, started undoing his bed, I kissed Jan and his still-warm feet goodbye and left the room. I drove around aimlessly for some time before returning home. Home was an empty, cold shell without Jan, a mausoleum. His things, his furniture, his "knick-knacks," his favourite chairs, records and books—I didn't see any of *my* belongings, everything was Jan's. *Without him* was coming at me, magnified with the speed and intensity of an express train. The emptiness of my life without him had no appeal or meaning.

If it hadn't been for my family, who rallied tightly around me, I think I would have surely died of a broken heart. In the days that followed, I functioned like an automaton, there were so many things that had to be attended to. First of all, the practical arrangements for the funeral, burial, and other red tape precipitated by such a tremendous change in one's life had to be attended to. I insisted on being included in all the details and arrangements. I didn't want to be spared, and as not to dwell on the enormity of the loneliness of an empty life before me, I wanted to be so busy so that I would have no time to think about it.

My husband, my lover, my friend, my confidant, my advisor, my protector, my stronger, better half was gone—my Camelot was no more. That part of our being that was essentially *ours* in marriage disintegrated by his death. What remained was too shattered by the grief, wounded beyond redemption, it seemed.

The final day came, two days before Christmas, when we put Jan to rest. Numbed to the core of my body, my face stiff from drying tears that flowed incessantly, I looked up across Jan's casket.

Dream sweet dreams my Love...

until we meet again.

Gone Is My Camelot

There, a little bit away to the left, stood a tall, white-robed figure that looked so much like Jesus and the message came to me with lightning clarity. Although the Lord brought me down, not only to my knees but right down flat onto my face, He also was there with me. Revelation to me was plain and explicit. The course of my new life had been clearly charted for me already, a long time ago, I must live it out according to the mission that had been bestowed upon me at the baptismal font.

Freed from original sin by being anointed with chrismal oil and holy water, I was joined irrevocably to the mystical body of Christ—his Church. Nothing and no one on earth can sever that bond to change my destiny. Through eyes that brimmed with free-flowing tears, I didn't notice at first that the Jesus figure in my vision had short hair. This Jesus figure, of course, was our Reverend, our young, beautiful priest, who anointed Jan when giving him his Last Rites a week ago in the hospital and now was blessing him for the last time before the interment.

I expressed my anguish in some measure in the letter of appreciation that I wrote to the hospital and the newspaper at the time:

> There are no adequate words to describe the agony of watching someone one loves suffering, being gravely ill and dying. At the same time, one experiences awe and amazement at witnessing, first-hand, a team of experts in action who, in the name of medical science, is doing everything that is humanly possible to save that patient.
>
> I know, I was there for almost three weeks before Christmas with my husband Jan, who was fighting desperately for his life in Room 224 at M.S.A. General Hospital. Jan had only a slim chance of recovery, having gone through radical lung surgery for cancer early in 1991, followed by extensive radiotherapy treatments. Nevertheless, he received the best of care from the very first day that he entered the hospital. For that, my family and I are very grateful. Through the many hours that I spent on the ward I often felt someone's arm around me and found a shoulder to cry on. I have seen tears of compassion and understanding in their eyes also. What my family and I will always remember about that sad time is the generous and genuine spirit of caring shown by the staff towards my husband and all our family. They helped to ease our pain and always reminded me that we were not alone.

Time Was Passing. . . .

It is more than two years now since Jan died. The pain of my loss is still with me and strong but it is not so acute or so raw anymore.

I still think about him all the time, each day and night and when I pray for him. But the memories of him aren't as poignant as before and even loneliness has become kinder and warmer. I have stopped looking for him around every corner and have stopped listening for his footsteps. My heart doesn't miss a beat when I see a man in the distance who resembles Jan or has some feature similar to Jan's. I have learned how not to prepare food for the two of us or shop for the things that he liked best. I stopped hurting so deeply, whether by simply accepting my lot with equanimity, or that my nervous system just got calloused by so much pain.

By now, I have resigned myself to widowhood and gotten used to being alone, and best of all, stopped feeling sorry for myself. Before, I would wince visibly, my eyes filling with tears at the sight of couples on the street or shopping together—now I don't even notice them anymore. Living with the family helps. There is so much comfort in having children close by, being tuned in to the hustle and bustle of normal everyday family living, that it takes my mind off the brooding.

A great deal has changed in other areas of my life, especially my spiritual life. After twenty years of religious hibernation and spiritual drought I was brought back into the fold by that young priest who so resembled Jesus (maybe not Jesus the Nazarene, but more like an actor playing the part).

The day after Jan died, Mary (Jan's sister), and I went to see Father Alan at St. Ann's Church in Abbotsford to make funeral arrangements for Jan. Father Alan knew already about my problems with non-attendance at Mass and other religious problems. As was expected of him, he strongly suggested that at such painful times there is a great comfort to be found in prayer and reconciliation with the Church, and that this can also speed the healing process. He made an appointment for Mary, Jan's sister, and I to come and see him the next day. Needless to say, I kept my appointment. How does one confess after a twenty-year break from religious observance? We spent close to half an hour in the reconciliation room and I cried

Coming Home

most of that time. Father Alan talked to me (and he is a gifted
speaker) about the futility of closing one's mind and soul to the
Church's teachings and God's love and grace that is bestowed on
each of us at baptism and that turning away from God equals
damnation. Seeing how wounded, exhausted, broken, and contrite

I was, he forgave me my sins in the name of Jesus Christ without hearing details about them.

Although sympathetic and compassionate, he was uncompromising in his demands of me. He wanted my firm commitment to return to the Church and her ministry without delay. I promised to return and have never looked back. Not that I found it always easy to stick to my commitments.

There was so much I had to learn; there have been many changes in the Church since the time I was a regular churchgoer. I needed so much more knowledge, even about simple Church observances in English, and the things that I knew about religion needed constant validation. There were so many questions I wanted to ask, so many doubts in my mind to dispel, and so much confusion to clarify and absolutely no one to turn to except Father Alan, whom I saw once a week at the Church during Mass or outside the Church to shake hands and say hello. I made appointments and saw him once or twice to seek his counsel. On his advice, and with Krys' encouragement, I joined the Catholic Woman's League, Bible study and catechism classes for adults. These activities kept me busy, happy, and satisfied my yearning for a more purposeful life. I learned how to pray effectively, made many wonderful new friends, and slowly but surely began the healing process on the road to recovery.

Once I focused on God and the spiritual aspects of my relation to Him in prayer, a slow but tremendous transformation took place in and around me. The slightest nuances of religious life previously unnoticed by me, took on a new meaning and perception in the depth of my feelings. Awareness of events that had taken place 2,000 years ago acquired a new dimension. The picture of life of the Holy Family, the life and ministry of Jesus that had been a flat, colourless image in my mind before, became animated and illuminated in beautiful colours. As if all the figures of people from biblical times, animals and the landscape, stepped out of the frame and set into motion a movie with lights, sound, voices, and music.

Panorama that had been stationary began moving around me. The most significant and exciting aspect of it is that I play my part in it also. My humble, sometimes mundane everyday life is my God-given role, no matter how small. My little part is still an important segment in the whole drama of creation that was written and is being produced and directed by the Creator Himself. Humanity was rescued from damnation and its salvation secured with the blood of God's Son, Jesus Christ. This holy drama is orchestrated and watched over by the Blessed Trinity, to ensure that the Pilgrim Church arrives safely at is final destination, to complete the pattern of His master plan in the realm of His kingdom with Jesus Christ and the queen of heaven, Mary the holy mother of God. Our part in God's scheme of things is to follow Jesus' example and live as He taught us, to the best of our potential. It seems easy and simple enough, providing that we open our hearts and souls to God with love, humility, unconditional surrender, trust, and submission to His will.

I feel now that, when the time comes for me to face my second coming be it personal or universal, I will be prepared.

CHAPTER NINE
Where Is God?

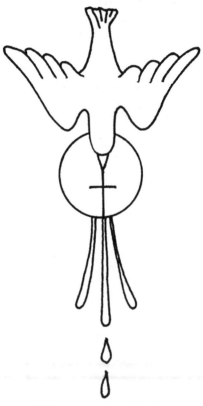

"Where were you, God . . . ?"

Where were you, God, all this time when the drama of my life was being played out? You couldn't have been too far away, since you made me and the invisible link between us has existed from the moment of my conception. The link with my mother had been severed at the time of my birth, but the link with you, Father, remained intact. In fact, it grew longer and stronger as I grew older, bolder, and more ignorant of your ways, but no matter what predicament I was in, I always felt you, omnipresent.

Even at my birth, God, when I was so weak and sickly you would not let me go. Beats me if I can fathom your mysterious reasons, why you had to put me through some of the exercises at all, but who am I to question your divine actions?

Later, although you let my mother die, you gave me three loving sisters who were willing and happy to take care of me. You truly cared what happened to me, Lord, by seeing that my earthly father was loving and crafty enough to put food on our table and clothes on our backs. You made me strong by letting me play those rough games with my brothers and their friends. You made me fearless of heights and deep waters. You have been really lenient toward me, Lord, by letting me wander around for so long a time, allowing me to use my free will to the fullest, when I was straining and stretching the link between us, indiscriminately and with impunity.

You see, Lord, to be truthful I was so ignorant I really didn't know you that well at the beginning. So, I was searching for you and the truth all those years by trial and error. We were formally introduced for the first time when I was about five years old. I clearly remember that instant, so I must have been past my infancy by then. My sister, Wala, told me to kneel down on the bed as the floor was too cold. Facing the wall, she pointed her finger towards the ceiling and said that up there was God, our Father, who made us and loves us and that we must pray to Him and worship Him. She made me repeat after her the Lord's Prayer, the Hail Mary and the Glory Be To The Father. We prayed like that for several evenings, until I memorized the prayers and could say them by myself. I climbed up into the loft, later, to investigate and see if you were there, God. To my great disappointment, there was nothing that resembled the face of a man that Wala showed me in her prayer book. No matter, I took Wala's word for it. How faithfully I practiced Wala's minsitrations I can't truthfully recall, Father, but lacking supervision and example, I am sure that I neglected my duties to you, Lord.

Later, of course, we were reintroduced during catechism classes in preparation for my first Holy Communion. By introducing me to your son's mission for humanity in the Holy Eucharist, you revealed to me the sacred inheritance that was offered to me from the cross for my salvation. By receiving my first Holy Communion, I should have been growing and thriving spiritually but I was too young and too alone in this venture, God.

Don't ask me Lord why my family didn't practice religion (you, of course, know all about it, anyway) because I don't know and none of them are alive to be questioned now. Without placing blame on anyone in particular, I can say that my religious training was sketchy to say the least, until that part of my life spent in Africa, where you, Lord, put me in a "training camp," so to speak, where I was subjected to rigorous practices of religious instruction in school, church, and at home.

My education came somewhat late, but was providential. You protected me Lord from disease and starvation when that cataclysmic hole of war and deprivation opened over your land. You fed me and kept me warm during that terrible train journey to Siberia. You helped me to overcome all the difficulties of learning a new language, and to deal with the adversity that surrounded me in school. You made me proud and strong, despite my humble circumstances. When I was hungry, cold and poorly dressed, I never complained or cried when I was laughed at. You sent that old Kazakh to retrieve me from that snowy grave when I was beaten and pushed out of the breadline. When he carried me on his back to safety, it was you, Lord, in the guise of that old man. You, Father, gave me strength to fight that attacker in Uzbekhistan, filling his wild heart with pity so he would let me go. You shaded my father, brother, and me from the hot sun in the desert, protected us from scorpions and snake bites, and held laughing jackals and hyenas at bay. You gave us enough strength to survive that last, long stretch when the three of us wandered around lost. At the height of our exhaustion, you sent us that wagon and those two men who gave us a lift, so we could reach the safety of our army who were on the point of leaving for Persia. The timing was too perfect as to be just a coincidence. Later again, Lord, you filled my brother's emaciated body with superhuman strength to enable him to chase the army convoy who left without us in the darkness of night, somewhere in the desert of Uzbekhistan. He caught up with them and begged for one of the horse-drawn wagons to come back and pick us up from the roadside ditch. How could they have found us without your guidance, Lord, in that wasteland and by the light of one hurricane lamp? You cared for me, cheered me, and warmed me, helped me to find food that sustained us. You protected me from all those dreadful diseases that were rampant and cutting down multitudes of people around me. I was never sick until we reached Teheran and the safety of good hospitals, good doctors, and nutrition, and even then, you pulled me through, Lord, when I asked you humbly.

Why, Lord, did you send us on yet another pilgrimage after the war was over? There must have been a very important plan in your "scheme of things." While the rest of the nations enjoyed their freedom, we lost our country again. The answer for that move never came to me—I am still waiting.

As the years went by, my relations with you, God, were somewhat lukewarm. I talked with you twice a day, attended Sunday masses, went to confession and even received communion, once in a while. Regular communion taken at every mass attended hadn't been practised in my early days. During our courtship with Jan, I tried to make a positive influence on him about religion in preparation for bringing up our future family according to the Catholic faith in a proper spiritual environment. For several years, everything progressed as it should, Lord. We were married in church, Krys was baptised, and I started taking her to church when she was two years old, although younger children were never taken to church in our community. When she was five you helped us to get her into a convent school so she could have a better basis for her religious life; that school was reputable and not easy for just anyone to get in. She attended catechism classes, received her first Holy Communion and was confirmed when we came to Canada. There didn't seem to be a single reason for a cloud to appear on our horizon, but one did, Lord, and you know that.

As the years went by, my difficulties in taking Jan and Krys to church increased. According to men of my generation Lord, going to church was for women and old people; men attended church on special occasions only. I had to be very careful to make sure that everyone in our family was in a good mood by Sunday so we could go to mass together. It wore me down and was really pointless, but I persisted. You gave me strength and hope, Lord. Until one day when Krys was seventeen, she asked me if going to all this trouble by taking her Dad and her to church was worth it. "Are you doing this for my benefit or yours?" she asked. Good Lord! A question like that coming from a girl who had spent four years in convent school in England and five years in Catholic schools in North Vancouver shook me badly. When my breath and speech returned, I answered as gently as I could that it was for both our benefits. She shook her head sadly then and returned as gently that I should carry out the duties to myself and not worry about her. She was old enough to make her own decisions and she didn't believe in any of this religious stuff, anyway. Jan didn't take sides on this, he remained neutral. Something snapped inside me then, that was that!

For the next twenty years, we didn't practice religion. Why, God, why did you let this happen? Such a terrible waste! Our mode of life didn't change, we were a happy, normal family, law-abiding, decent citizens. Jan and I even prayed to you, Father, daily, and we didn't preach anything new, we just stopped practicing religion. I felt guilt and shame about our abandonment of the church, but I didn't do anything about it either; that was my dilemma and my tragedy. You, God, were so patient with me for such a long time. Twenty years—it is a lifetime for some people, but as all earthly things end, this situation had to come to an end, also. Enough was enough—Lord, you jerked on the invisible chain between us so hard that I staggered and fell down to my knees at my husband's deathbed. Yes, Lord, I saw your stern face in my dying husband's face. Jan's face was so solemn, so serious, so set and unmoving, and so *uncompromising*—he was going on his way despite my begging. This pilgrim now had heard your call, Lord, he reached his final destination, he faced the second coming in the here and now. I was chilled to my bones. I was crushed, defeated, helpless. I heard your verdict then upon me, an order to mend my ways and to help others do likewise.

Yes, Lord, I am willing and able to do your will, just show me the way and please, please grant me grace, strength, wisdom and light of the Holy Spirit.

Where Is God?

I don't think that this question can be answered by only one individual because there will probably be as many different answers as there are people on this earth. I personally find you, Lord, everywhere, within me and around me. Anything that I look at, touch, or think about in it I see the wonders of your great creative powers. I see you in the unfathomable phenomena of the ever-changing seasons that come about with such regularity, purpose, design and perfect order. I see you in the light of the sun and in the moon, in the days and nights. I see you, Lord, in the midnight blue firmament on a peaceful night studded with starry constellations, and in the pale amber of dawn and the deep orange hues of sunset that flood the heavens above. I hear you, Lord, in the birds' chorus that explodes in the predawn hosanna, and in the evening; in the sweet whispers of benedictions. I see your benign, mighty face in the white fluffiness of clouds that float across crystal blue shimmering skies. I see you in the fast-flowing creeks and in the slow-winding rivers, in the expanse of the oceans and in the deep, peaceful lakes. I see you in the streams that come tumbling down the mountainsides and in the high, craggy mountain peaks, with their wide alpine meadows and forests below. I see you, Lord, in the emerald expanse of grasses that sway gracefully in the wind, and in the colourful symphony of the floral carpet that covers your kingdom's endless meadows and fields. With trembling heart I listen to the tempest of wrath and fury of the storms and gale force winds that you send upon this land, a reminder to people of your might. I see you and hear you in the universal silence of a deep winter landscape and in the quivering air on a hot, summer day.

I can go on and on and on, singing your praises; the litany of your glory, love, and greatness is as endless as infinity, Lord. You are everything and everywhere, you are the universe! I am so close to you that I can feel your presence, I can almost touch you, and for me just to think that I am an integral part of this, your creation, takes my breath away and fills me with awe and amazement. Thoughts that I am a humble result of your might and love make me tremble. When I close my eyes, I can see the image of you and all people on earth, like one gigantic, immense, immeasurable rosary.

The chain is made up of our souls connected to the cross that is you, Lord; the beads are our bodies. At the end of our individual path on earth, as our body expires, the bead splits and falls off the chain. The chain, our soul, remains connected to you Lord, forever. It is at the cross that we profess our credo to you and your infinite existence, Lord, each time we say the rosary. Everything that you created and that your son, Jesus Christ, established on this earth for

The Rosary

us to follow for our salvation is one universal pilgrimage. Your love and your mercy embrace us all. The grace of your divine being fills our souls abundantly in answer to our prayer, humility, acts of deep devotion, submission and total surrender to your fatherly care. Responding to your call, Father, we pilgrims—your Church, the Mystical Body of Christ—travel relentlessly "until that day comes when with the saints we may praise you forever."

Forgive me, Lord, if I didn't present my theory of your whereabouts in a better, more profound way, but that is all the inspiration that I receive from you, Father. I can only express my devotion in this somewhat inadequate way.

CHAPTER TEN
A New Beginning

The bright, sunny summer day was approaching its end. The light-blue western sky was suffused with crimson rays of the fiery, orange globe of the slowly sinking sun. What can there be more beautiful than the ending of a warm June day over the Polish countryside? Peace and quiet prevailed over the vast woodlands, meadows, and fields of the fleeting landscape. Here and there, herds of cattle, finally satisfied with the lush, green grass of the pasture rested sleepily, lazily chewing their cud. It seemed that even people, after an arduous day of activity, slow their pace and relish with satisfaction and tranquility the ending of yet another productive day.

The Berlin-Vilnius night express train raced relentlessly eastward, oblivious to all this surrounding beauty. In the first sleeper compartment number four, two figures sat quietly. One of them was watching the passing kaleidoscope with great concentration, absorbed completely in every detail, thirstily drinking in the beauty of each passing moment. The other figure, with a Mona Lisa smile on her lips, watched her enchanted companion with a motherly indulgence.

Yes, my niece Janka, my sister Wacia's daughter, and nine years my junior, had lived in Poland all her life and had visited our birthplace four times in the past. Janka, who never left her country, was never ravaged by war and deportation. Never having experienced hunger and a burning longing to return to her homeland, she couldn't possibly fathom the emotions that were devouring me. Besides, she sat there quietly, allowing me the chance to live it all out without interruption. Also, by then she was tired; we both were tired after having gone through the nerve-wracking experience of getting *on* the train in the first place.

While I was enjoying a breathtaking week-long holiday with my other niece, Zosia, and her husband, Heniek, in a spa town on the Baltic Sea called Miedzyzdroje, Janka was supposed to make all the arrangements necessary for our trip East. A clerk at the travel bureau, *Orbis in Zielona Gora,* informed her that there was no need to obtain tickets beforehand. All we had to do was to tell officials on entering the train that we were paying for our tickets with American dollars—the "almighty dollar" indeed.

Well, not everything was as simple as that. Mietek, Janka's husband, drove us to Zbaszynek, which is in the southwestern corner of Poland about twenty four kilometres from their homes in Sulechow. A stony faced official in the ticket office told us that she had never heard of such a tenuous arrangement before, and that as far as she was concerned, it was very difficult to get on the Berlin-Vilnius train without tickets and reservations. "The Berliner-Vilnius arrives here usually full-up," she told us woodenly. Our eager hearts dropped to the soles of our feet on hearing that statement. Our final and only solution was to "just wait and see." Mietek kept teasing us and making Jasia angrier by the minute. He kept reassuring us that he would drive us back home without charge. The fact that there was only one more gentleman near us and a group of teeangers on the far end of the platform gave us hope and encouragement.

Two conductors who had just passed us and sat down on a bench nearby, and were immediately accosted for information by Jasia, weren't any more forthcoming. Yes, they were going to get on that train; yes, they were going to be in charge, but NO they were NOT selling ANY tickets. They also told her that there was always a person in charge of each wagon, a civilian, usually a Russian who ushers passengers in and takes care of all their needs in his/her jurisdiction. He/she issues each passenger their bedding and towels, provides tea and dry snacks for the duration of the journey.

Jasia knew all about that already from her previous trips on different lines. In spite of all the mournful predictions, we were trying to look and behave cheerfully—bright, brave smiles never left our faces. Finally, at 1500 hours sharp, the eagerly awaited Berlin-Vilnius train: huffing, puffing, screeching, and hissing rolled slowly into the station and stopped, with those two wagons reserved for Vilnius right in front of us. Doors opened at once and there he stood: "Mr. Clean" in all his glory, glaring down on us. He only differed in appearance from the original by a hat he wore: a pair of blue jeans and a crew-cut instead of a bald pate and white T-shirt and pants.

Brave Janka pushed me towards the door and following closely behind me, asked one of our conductors to introduce us to "Mr. Clean." A magic password must have been exchanged (probably in U.S. dollars) between the two of them because "Mr. Clean" moved quickly to the side and helped me to get into the train. There were a great number of compartments to choose from, as the train was almost empty. Besides the two of us, there were two young gentlemen (nationality unknown) and one German couple. Within a few minutes our "Mr. Clean" appeared, delivering two packages of bedding containing a blanket, two linen sheets, one towel, one pillowcase and an upholstered foam pillow. What else could two stowaways wish for? We quickly made our beds on the lower benches in case the train picked up a crowd later on.

And so, our sweet soap opera began without a hitch, until Warsaw, where we were rolled up and down the railway tracks for about an hour, collecting all the wagons heading east and arriving from all over the country. Sometime later, one of the conductors collected our fees up to Warsaw in *zlotys*—420,000—but he never issued us any tickets. From Warsaw to Vilnius, we paid twenty two dollars each to "Mr. Clean," who conveniently delayed issuing the tickets until our arrival in Vilnius. There, Jasia went to his compartment to ask for his help to get a box down containing a microwave oven that we were delivering to our contact in Vilnius, but more about that later.

Right now, while I was still transported into another world, marvelling in my reverie, Janka lost her interest in watching me, and prompted by the more natural instinct of hunger, went in search of some tea so that we could have our supper of ham sandwiches, fruit, candies and lemonade that we had brought from home. Finally, mission accomplished, she arrived armed with two large glasses of tea, Russian style. Russians drink their tea clear in glasses which are nestled in ornamental metal holders.

We had left Warsaw by then and while enjoying our picnic-like supper, we watched the slowly approaching twilight, falling softly over the everchanging panorama. Change came gradually but definitely, visibly apparent to the eye of the observer with each passing mile, moving towards the eastern part of Poland. Gone were the vast, lush, green fields of crops where every inch of ground is cultivated tenderly and used largely for growing vegetables, rye, oats, wheat, corn, and barley as well as pasturing cattle, the pride of the Polish farmer. Gone were the prize-winning cultivated flower fields and neat pens of different poultry and small farm animals. Gone were the wide, flat, open spaces with the dark, majestic forests full of ancient oaks and tall, white birches and pines on the horizon.

Instead, the land appeared as if it had undergone some geological upheaval during the formation of its crust, resulting in gentle, low hills and scant valleys filled with boggy marshlands, woods, copses and wasteland. The habitation matched the landscape. Small farms and hamlets prevailed over town and cities.

The warm, summer night eventually interrupted our nostalgic observations, wrapping her soft, velvety veils of darkness over a peacefully sleeping countryside.

When we arrived on the Polish border, it had turned completely dark. A one-hour time difference applies in Bialorussia and I was amazed and a little apprehensive about the number of uniformed army personnel who appeared to be busy doing the same thing. There were so many officials, all of them in military apparel, who were checking our passports and asking questions, *like what goods we were carrying?* It looked like the whole battalion ran past our door, looking in during our questioning. Young, lonely soldiers were probably eager to find young, beautiful girls to look at, but in the meantime, they made it appear like we were in a war zone with all their military activities.

The next thing that followed is notably typical of Russians; a procedure only experimented with in one or two other countries in the world. It was time to change the wheels and axle shafts on the train! Russian railway lines are wider and don't fit the trains of the rest of the neighbouring countries of Europe. The whole bizarre but amazing operation, which deserves a medal for the precision with which it is conducted, goes like this: In the small town called Kuznica-Bialowieska, the train is driven several kilometres outside town where it is then lifted up a few metres above the ground by special hydraulic lifts. A large group of skillfully trained engineers quickly, expertly, and without much fuss or disturbance change the wheels and axle shafts on the whole train. Then the train is lowered back onto the tracks and away it goes through the Bialoruss checkpoint and into Russian territory. The whole operation takes about two hours.

On the border in Grodno, while one officer scrutinized our passports, another asked us to leave our compartment. He concluded a thorough search inside, including the lifting of the seats to see if there were any arms, ammunition, or drugs that we were transporting. We arrived at the Lithuanian border checkpoint around 5:30 A.M. A cold wind was tossing heavy rainclouds around a low, grey sky. A solitary railway car border office perched precariously on the slope of the railroad. A wet, soggy Lithuanian flag flopped sadly in the wind. On one side of the car office there were two completely disbanded, grotesque-looking empty shells of tanks. They looked like two child's toys left beheind in a hurry.

Suddenly, a sharp knock: the door of our compartment opened and a Lithuanian border guard in a military uniform (again) appeared like a "Jack-in-a-box" smiling, wishing us "Good morning" in Russian and he asked us for our passports. A customs officer, as courteous as the guard, took even less time to ask us if we were carrying anything that should be declared. Receiving a negative reply, he saluted and closed the door behind him.

We finished our remaining sandwiches for an early breakfast and settled down happily for another snooze. Later, we watched the passing countryside, noting almost with regret the difference from the western to the eastern territory, where very little can be seen from the window of the train because the railway lines go through a "corridor" of pine forest, planted, it is said, deliberatley, to screen the railroad from heavy snow drifts during long, severe winters. Scathing rumour has it that the screen is also to prevent travellers from seeing what goes on in Soviet territory. A narrow belt between the forest and railroad is cultivated on both sides and is used for growing potatoes. Miles and miles on end of early potato crops run alongside the rail lines, their irregular and sparse plants giving true evidence of poor soil and cultivating practices inherited haphazardly from the "kolhoz" days of communal farming. We arrived in Vilnius as scheduled at 10:00 A.M. on June 16, 1994.

The next day, we travelled from Vilnius to my birthplace, to revisit my golden days, the distant place of my dreams. First we went to Swir, about a 100-kilometre journey from Vilnius and there we found ourselves grounded. My golden days! . . . The distant place of my dreams. So near and yet so far away, one and a half kilometres as the crow flies and about five kilometres on the road from Swir. Road? What road? After travelling on a very badly damaged and left unrepaired road as far back as the Lithuanian border, suddenly there appeared a moonscape of sandy-clay ditches many of which were filled with muddy water from the recently

105

fallen rain. There was no mistake, it was Swir, our peaceful little town from the memory of my distant childhood. There was the church, post office, pharmacy, the little shops and hard cobblestone streets that I remember so clearly. Now, what faced us was my nightmare.

With my eyes opened in full daylight I was dreaming an ugly dream that we were grounded on the doorstep of our destination. As we were approaching Swir, we passed the cemetery, the resting place of my mother and in the distance I saw our church nestled among the tall trees. My expectant, eager heart swelled with pride. This was the church where I was baptized on the day that I was born and where later I celebrated my first Holy Communion.

Now, just before the church, there stood a formidable-looking barricade blocking our progress. The "detour" sign with its friendly looking arrow, the mandatory sign that appears before the frustrated motorist in Canada, was nowhere in sight. There was no such luxury here, we didn't even have a choice. With thick woods on our left, we could either turn back or plunge our car into the pot-holed dirt lane frequented only by giant military vehicles. Our church, our beautiful, old church, looked desolate, a desecrated place, its doors firmly shut and its interior now used for the storage of old junk.

Anything that could go wrong that day, did. The twinge of apprehension that I was feeling from the moment we arrived in Vilnius bore its fruit. The spectre of imminent disaster materialized. Yesterday, Raymond (my sister Wercia's grandson) met us at the station in Vilnius and drove us to the tiny bachelor apartment that he shares with his girlfriend, Iringa. She was at work and Raymond, who is an accomplished chef, prepared and served us our breakfast. I had never met Raymond before and was very touched by seeing him. Here, I thought, is something of Wercia, my sister, to meet us, and the thought gave me a warm feeling inside. His welcome was unmistakably friendly for both of us, but with my sixth sense I detected some slight constraint in him. Something was wrong and the feeling made me uneasy.

106

I was right—later, on our return trip to Vilnius we learned that the timing of our arrival had not been exactly convenient for Raymond, who had neglected to mention this little detail to Jasia when she was making arrangements with him for our meeting. He was going to his cousin's wedding in Swienciany, seventy kilometres away from Vilnius in direction of Swir. Jasia and I descended on him on the 16th of June, the day before he was scheduled to leave. Who could blame Ray for feeling frustrated, but how were we supposed to know about his previous engagement?

My Lithuanian visa was for a month's duration and for Bialoruss for twenty days. Jasia, as a Polish-passport holder, didn't need a visa to travel anywhere in Europe. Our trip to Vilnius could have been changed by a few days either way. A lack of communication between us created this peculiar situation. Raymond had to be crafty enough to try to be in both places at the same time. Right, good luck!

After our breakfast, Raymond offered to drive us to the supermarket to meet his mother where she works and to take care of some errands. He had actually outdone himself because after the supermarket, he took us on a sightseeing tour of the town. I never expected this extra treat on the day of our arrival and didn't even take my camera with me. Ray told me not to worry, that he would take us there again. Later that day, Jasia and Raymond informed me that we were leaving on our trip down my memory lane tomorrow morning. The urgency and haste of a decision made without consulting me surprised and unsettled me a little, but who was I to argue? I was just a visitor here, ready to comply with the plans of my hosts, who knew best.

Early the next day, bright-eyed and excited, we left home. Having dropped Iringa at the bank where she works, we turned down the hundred-kilometre-long road to my "Waterloo." The weather was nothing to brag about, it was cold and windy with intermittent clouds and showers—depressing enough. After an hour of a very bumpy ride we reached the border. Roads in Poland

107

are bad and they get increasingly worse with each passing mile heading eastward.

The Lithuanian military border guards gave us no problem. After checking our passports they waved us across the netural zone towards the Bialoruss checkpoint, where we received our first crushing blow. "No one can cross our border without a visa, including Polish passport holders," said the guard to our astonished faces. "No one!" was his final, adamant reply, contrary to what we had been told at the Bialoruss embassy in Warsaw, where Jasia and I had gone a month earlier to get Lithuanian and Bialoruss visas for me. There the official had told Jasia that there is no need for a visa for Polish passport holders. Who was right? The embassy in Poland or this guard here?

Angry and frustrated, Jasia and Raymond got out of the car. Earnest pleas and explanations didn't impress the guard. The touching argument that their old aunt (indicating me) had travelled all the way from Canada to visit her mother's grave made no difference. We could not cross their border. That was final. Brave Jasia was truly brave this time. She told them what nobody would ever dare tell them before *Perestroika* that they were out of their minds and that she was going to write to Warsaw to file a formal complaint about their incompetence.

"Niet, Niet, Niet!" was as firm as "niet" could ever be. She remained undefeated, however, and said that they could detain her here but they must let Raymond and me go across. "But, of course," said the guard "the Canadian and Lithuanian are free to go. They have our visa. You stay here with us in our office." The office was located in the old railway car. "You must provide me with caviar, vodka and good coffee," was Jasia's parting shot as they led her away. The border barrier in front of us lifted slowly and we drove into the lion's den, Raymond cursing softly under his breath and I with sinking heart.

Now we were in Swir, obviously defeated by natural forces. While Raymond sweating profusely and huffing and puffing, tried to cross the obstacles of the detour between small, grey, dilapidated houses whose murky, little windows almost touch the ground, I was sitting all tensed up and trembling, holding on desperately to my seat and praying silently that nothing would break down. With each bump of the undercarriage against the ground, I tensed more and rose from my seat. By the time we reached the other end of the barricade, I was sick to my stomach. In actual fact, I was ill, although I didn't realize it at the time. When, on our return from the trip, I went to see a doctor, my blood pressure was 180/100. With a dose of the hypertension drug that I had inside me it was frightening enough but right now, with heavy, rapid beats of my heart and tears in my eyes I stared horrified, at the desolate scene of neglect and abandonment, in complete disbelief. These depressing fragments before me somehow didn't match the scenes of my imagined Utopia. Damn my vivid fantasies and my idealized past. I had formed a completely different picture of my homeland in my mind.

A clear vision: I would be standing there amidst the green, lush meadows, forests, and pastures that had surrounded our home. A midday sun would pour molten gold over the countryside, asleep in the noon heat. The lazy drone of a bumblebee crawling in and out of the cup of a wild rose filled my ear. Even the tiny dot of a lark, high in the crystal blue sky and sprinkling the brilliant tones of his Gloria, sending them straight to the Almighty: This was the picture in my mind.

Well, what I was staring at was cold reality and it wasn't pretty. I wanted to take a picture of the poor old church with its peeling paint, cracked doors and weatherbeaten walls but quickly put my camera behind my back when I saw two giant military trucks rolling towards us. We got into the car and drove carefully away. Raymond tried to reassure me that those trucks weren't military trucks anymore and only civilians drove them now for private cartage and that I could have taken a photograph of the church without any repercussions. The spire of the church was still visible from where we were, so I took a picture of that.

My cup wasn't overflowing yet but more was still ahead. Coming this way, we decided that the best way to visit my mother's grave would be on our return trip. We parked our car opposite the cemetery and crossed the road. Raymond opened an old, sad-looking gate. *Turn left as you enter the cemetery.* I heard my father's distant words in my head and *under the first old pine tree is your mother's grave.* I found the tree and I found my mother's resting place. It was a pile of cemetery refuse, a mound overgrown with sparse, anemic grass. In place of a headstone a dirty, rusty old bucket had been placed turned upside down.

The picture of derision and condemnation was complete. Why God? Why this final humiliation? Was it retribution? Did I tempt fate too far, coming from across the world? Was I too proud about this whole episode? Was I idolizing and maybe overreacting about this whole thing? Finally, why did my older sisters not take better care of our mother's grave?

Wercia had lived in Swieciany all her life, only a few kilometres away from here and died in 1986. Wala had lived in Poland, visited Wercia occasionally and died in 1988. Neglect of the grave was at least half a century old. I left the grave and cemetery in a state of emotional turmoil. Raymond closed the gate, I took a picture of the pine tree and we drove away. My pilgrimage to revisit "my golden days of summer" was over. The anticlimax was great and totally unexpected.

Even though I was truly sick with a blinding headache and waves of nausea, I felt somehow greatly relieved. It had been like an awakening from a long sleep filled with nightmares. Or, like getting over a serious surgery and coming to after an anaesthetic. The pain was still there, but also gladness and relief that the operation was over. All my mature life there had been something deep inside me that was constantly weeping slow, bitter tears of longing and resentment for the fate that had befallen us both as a nation and as a family. The gnawing, corrosive feeling inside me that could only be compared to a chronic heartburn had always been there but now it was gone. I was really thirsty, tired and dizzy by now, but I felt lighthearted too, somehow, almost happy and in a strange way, fulfilled. Is this possible?

Raymond, oblivious of my inner storm of emotions, and prompted by his own private problems, pressed hard on the accelerator. We soon reached the border. When passing Lyntupy I had taken a picture of a beautiful church there. Raymond asked me if I wanted to visit that infamous station from which we had departed on February 10, 1940. I said "No" without a moment's hesitation and with glee in my voice. I wasn't going to see Lyntupy's station or anything else of that kind. I wouldn't torture myself with the macabre details of my distant past anymore. I was on my return trip from the past; I had to do it or drive myself mad with empty recriminations and regrets. I am the youngest and only remaining family member and I was going to lay all the ghosts of the past to rest and leave everything behind me—that was my final resolution.

Jasia, tired but unharmed, was glad to see us. Without further complications, we left the border and headed towards Swieciany where Raymond wanted to see his cousins and show us my sister Wercia's and her husband's resting place. After placing some flowers we brought from Raymond's cousin's store on Wercia's grave, we drove back to Vilnius. As soon as we started on our way, Raymond said haltingly that the girl we had met at the store was his cousin and that he was invited to her wedding, but that, of course, he had refused the invitation. They had spoken Lithuanian in the store so we didn't know what had transpired during their conversation. Surprised by his words, I swallowed hard and looked at him helplessly. Jasia, however, didn't have my scruples. "What's the problem?" she said. "Go to the wedding with our blessing. Take us to Vilnius and come back here at once. We have your apartment at our disposal and I know Vilnius. We will be perfectly contented on our own." Raymond didn't need this message repeated.

When we arrived in Vilnius, he prepared and served us dinner then put a few of his belongings together and drove happily away. Iringa went to visit her parents for the weekend and Jasia and I settled down to enjoy our solitude. Later, we went for a walk and did some shopping. Next day, Raymond's mother, (another Janka), took us under her wing. We went to the marketplace with her to have a look around and buy souvenirs. In the afternoon she drove us to her *dacha* on the outskirts of Vilnius where we spent a pleasant, restful afternoon.

Raymond returned late on Sunday afternoon, tired but happy and full of news to share with his mother. The next day, he took us on a shopping spree and a sightseeing tour. Later that afternoon, mother and son saw us off at the railway station and we departed from Vilnius at 1700 hours.

Our return trip was accomplished without any unusual incidents, the same old routine only in reverse. Again, we had a compartment to ourselves in an almost empty wagon. After all the border controls were over, including the changing of the wheels, we retired for the night. Around 5:00 A.M. I was awakened by an unusual light coming through the gap of the window curtains. Careful so as not to wake Jasia, who was snoring gently on the bench, I pushed my curtain aside. I looked out curiously and what I saw too my breath away.

In front of me was a scene of ghostlike quality. A large area, a meadow with trees, bushes and many other objects was swimming in a sea of early morning mist that was rising from the damp, warm ground. The sky was the palest pale green, darker high above and gradually getting paler towards the east and finally changing into palest pink and yellow right above the horizon. I was delighted that I was a witness to the miracle of the birth of a new day. With childlike amazement, I gazed at a sun that wouldn't rise. I never saw a rising sun at this hour before and didn't know how long it took the sun to rise.

The train was racing fast in the opposite direction and the unevenness of the terrain was screening the sight of the sun from me now and again. One moment, I would see a bright, yellow aura gleaming and flowing from side to side, touching the horizon only then to recede, as if extinguished again. On the opposite side, high in the sky scattered clouds were bathed in the glory of a deep-red reflection of the sun that wouldn't rise. Finally, after an hour of this tremendous play of the celestial elements, the fiery giant ball rolled slowly up.

Glory Allelujah! The mighty monarch had risen from his bed. The first day of summer was born, June 21, 1994. For the first time in my life, I said my morning prayers *facing* the rising sun. From the phenomenon I had just witnessed I took a message for myself, a firm resolution to make a change, a definite turn in my life; to close the chapter of my somewhat-shattered life and put it away, lovingly like an favourite old book and start a new day, a new chapter.

There had been too many traumatic upheavals in my life; the most recent, shattering and wounding one being the loss of my husband. Something very vital, youthful, and beautiful in me died with him. I had changed and things would never be the same again. Our path, that we had treaded in companionable unison for forty one years, ended abruptly at the seashore and Jan sailed away on the phantom ship toward the distant shore, leaving me behind orphaned and somewhat damaged.

Recriminations and self-pity are counterproductive, corrosive, and useless. Thoughts of what might have been lead to a dead-end. I have to find enough strength and determination to look ahead and make my new life a happy one again, all by myself. Is it possible? Yes, I have been told so many times by so many people. Can a bird with a broken wing fly again? Yes, no, maybe? It may depend on the extent of my injury, my capacity, and will for healing. But a bird with a broken wing can walk, it can hop, it can even run, maybe a little awkwardly, and lopsidely. It can also feed and it can even hide from dangers, but best of all it can sing loudly and clearly—Glory to God in His heaven. In the final analysis, we all are the wounded healers on this earth.

Epilogue

Reflections on Poland

It is far easier to begin writing a book or even a short story than it is to write the ending of it. One's thoughts seem to go on and on, expanding on a topic rather than finding something that appropriately sums it up and closes the subject.

For me, to end my odyssey, it was necessary to return to my homeland where my tale begins, to close a magic circle and assuage the yearnings that had inspired me to write my story in the first place.

To go to Poland was easy; I had gone back there twice before, once in 1970, and once in 1989. Each time, I found Poland at a different political stage, in a different social climate. The state of affairs in Poland during my first visit was reminiscent of the strife of enemy occupation and police-state activities. There was no true freedom in any shape or form, even though the Soviets were so loudly proclaiming it during their "liberation" of Europe in 1945. The feeling of oppression, the constant looking over of one's shoulder was damning enough and the presence of a huge number of Soviet military wasn't comforting in the least. The Poles, my family included, had seemingly succumbed to the inevitable, doing their best under the circumstances in order to survive.

During my second visit in the spring of 1989—on the threshold of *Perestroika*—I found Poland in an entirely different mood. The euphoria of hope and change for the better gripped the nation, setting a fast pace for new reforms that would open a wide avenue to the free market and democracy.

In May 1994, I found myself in the middle of a whirlwind of great activity for private enterprise and the westernization in Poland. Poles, a hard-working, extremely resourceful and very ambitious people, are speeding forward to make changes at a tremendous rate in order to catch up with the West, in all areas of life. The gentle, thawing wind of change that blew from the East in 1989 had transformed itself into a strong, steady gale on Polish soil and is gathering momentum on its way to greater and greater achievements. Consumer goods are plentiful, beautiful, and of good quality. Stores and markets are full of every commodity one could wish for, including items imported from the West. Food is excellent and service unsurpassed. The popular saying these days in Russia is "If we want to go to America, all we have to do is cross the border into Poland."

The Polish people, are, however, greatly hampered by high unemployment, high taxes, and low wages, the usual ills brought on by the recession. The Polish economy, whose resources had been depleted and literally ruined by fifty years of tremendous abuse by Communist rule, will require a great many decades of resourcefulness to completely recover. The prognosis is good, however, and the morale and attitude of the individual citizen is encouraging.

Despite the usual friction and squabbling among politicians, peaceful coexistence prevails and people are busy doing their best to get ahead, and not trying to subdue each other by brute force. Being predominantly Catholic helps insofar as people that pray together are less likely to kill each other.

As for me, I came, I saw, and I definitely conquered, I managed to rid myself of what amounted to an obssession that had haunted me for far too long. I also came to the realization that Canada, my new motherland, has my love, respect, and undivided loyalty, despite my deep love for the country of my birth. Before I left for Poland I was seriously contemplating remaining living there permanently, but after two months I was too homesick to think of anything else but returning home to Canada. I *will* return to Poland at least one more time, to fulfill my obligation toward my mother by placing a memorial on her grave, but I will be simply a Canadian tourist.